Back from Boot Hill

Colin Bainbridge

A Black Horse Western

ROBERT HALE · LONDON

© Colin Bainbridge 2014
First published in Great Britain 2014

ISBN 978-0-7198-1189-0

Robert Hale Limited
Clerkenwell House
Clerkenwell Green
London EC1R 0HT

www.halebooks.com

Typeset by
Derek Doyle & Associates, Shaw Heath
Printed and bound in Great Britain by
CPI Antony Rowe, Chippenham and Eastbourne

CHAPTER ONE

The eyes of Clay Tulane flickered open to a profound darkness. He lay still for a few moments feeling almost content, lulled by a gentle swaying motion. Faint sounds entered his ears, dim and strangely muted. He was lying on his back but when he stretched his legs and made to turn over, he was instantly brought up against something hard. He tried the other way with the same effect. He lifted his head and it touched a solid surface. His hands were folded on his chest but they were free and he was able to feel his surroundings. He seemed to be confined in some sort of box.

Suddenly he felt panic rise to his throat. He knew without doubt that the box was a coffin. He was buried alive. Instinctively he made to sit upright; this time his head smashed against the coffin lid and he sank back again as blood trickled down his forehead. Breathing deeply, he struggled to gain control of himself. He was moving and there were sounds. He couldn't be underground. Not yet. But if he was in a coffin, he must be on his way to the cemetery. They were taking him to Boot Hill. He didn't know how it could have happened, but that was of no concern to him. It wouldn't take them long to reach their destination. They must be almost there. There was no time to waste. He needed to let someone know that he was still alive.

Raising his hands again, he began to push at the coffin lid but he couldn't get much purchase. The lid seemed to be fastened tight and he soon gave up the attempt. After a moment's thought he began to shout. The sound of his voice in the confined space was deafening and he felt certain that someone must hear him. He stopped and listened. There was no response. He started again, shouting as loud as he could, but when he ceased the result was the same. Panic once again threatened to overwhelm him and it took a big effort to stay firm.

He had just about got himself under control once more when the swaying motion came to a halt. His heart thumped. Someone must have heard him. He waited for some reaction but nothing happened and after a few moments the swaying started again, caused by the movement of the wagon which was taking him to the cemetery.

The wagon had stopped briefly before continuing its way, which probably meant they had reached the entrance. It couldn't be long till it stopped again and they began to lower him into the ground.

Why was no one responding? He realized his fingers were tightly gripped and he stretched them out, rubbing them against his trouser leg. He felt something cold and metallic and realized that he still had his gun.

Skip Malloy drew his wagon to a halt beside an open grave. He looked about him. Most of the people taking up space in Boot Hill he had buried himself. They were for the most part a fairly ornery bunch, those that he knew anything about. Others were strangers he had never seen till they ended up in his funeral parlour. Like the man he was about to bury now, once his assistant showed up. Where was the boy? He was late, but there was nothing unusual in that. It didn't bother him. He had learned to take life as it came and make the most of moments like this. He drew out a pouch of tobacco, rolled himself a cigarette and leaned back to enjoy the sunshine and the silence his deafness afforded. He had come to make a virtue of being hard of hearing too. It was the only way to get by.

He drew in the cigarette smoke, savouring the

taste and appreciating the way it caught at his throat. He felt reflective. That was the effect this place always had on him. He was contemplating making an effort to get down from his seat when the peace was shattered by an explosion even his ears couldn't fail to register.

Three shots in rapid succession rang out from just behind him, jerking him upright and causing the cigarette to fall from his mouth. The horse stepped forwards and he hauled on the reins.

'What in tarnation!' he muttered.

A further shot rang out and he sprang from the wagon seat as quickly as his knees would allow him. The shots were coming from the coffin, blasting holes in the lid from which tapers of smoke were ascending. Standing well back from the wagon he shouted in a loud and somewhat tremulous voice:

'Hold it! Stop the shootin' and I'll have you right out of there.' Out of the corner of his eye he saw the boy approaching. Despite himself, he was shaken and he felt relieved to see him.

'What happened?' the boy said as he came up to the wagon. 'I heard gunfire.' The oldster pointed at the coffin. 'Help me unscrew the lid,' he said.

With the boy's help and the aid of a screwdriver it took no time at all to loosen the lid. As they worked on it, the undertaker talked to the man inside, calming and reassuring him. He didn't want to take any further risks with the gun. They had almost finished the job when the coffin lid was thrust open from below, knocking the boy aside, and the occupant sat bolt upright. The undertaker, despite having had time to adjust to the situation, was taken aback. He made to say something but could only stare in bewilderment as Tulane climbed out of the coffin and jumped down from the wagon. He spent a few moments bending and stretching his legs before turning to the under-taker.

'Hell,' he said, 'what's goin' on here? I think you got some explainin' to do.' The oldster didn't reply. Tulane shook himself as the boy regained his feet.

'He can't hear you too well,' the boy replied, seeing a look of irritation appear on the erstwhile corpse's face. 'If you take it slow, he can read your lips.'

Tulane turned to him. 'Who are you?' he said.

'Folks call me Pocket,' the boy replied.

The undertaker, watching the exchange between the youngster and Tulane, seemed to understand. 'Like the name of the town,' he said. 'Water Pocket. Without the Water. He ain't got no family. No one knows his real name.'

Tulane turned to the boy. 'Well, Pocket,' he said, 'I guess I should really be thankin' you and. . . .'

He paused.

'Malloy, Skip Malloy,' the undertaker answered, responding to his prompting.

'And Mr Malloy. Sorry if I sounded a bit tetchy, but I reckon you'll agree it's understandable.' He held out his hand for the undertaker to grasp. 'The name's Tulane, Clay Tulane.'

'How come you ain't a corpse?' the boy muttered.

'That's sure what I would like to know.'

Malloy was sufficiently cognisant to know that some sort of explanation was expected. He also realized that, as the person who had put the stranger in the coffin, he was in an awkward situation.

'They brought you in dead,' he replied. 'Naturally, the marshal handed you on. Believe me, no one is more surprised than me. I just did what I had to do.'

Tulane's face was contorted in an effort at concentration. 'Who brought me in?' he asked.

'A couple of boys from the Bar Nothing.'

Tulane shook his head. 'Hell,' he said, 'that's appropriate. What did you say is the name of this town?'

'Water Pocket.'

'See, he's readin' your lips,' the boy commented.

'I don't understand any of this,' Tulane said.

10

The undertaker saw his chance. 'Why don't you and the boy get back up in the wagon and I'll drive us back to town?' he said. 'You can figure out what's best to do after that.'

Tulane continued to look puzzled but finally nodded his head. 'I guess that makes sense,' he said. 'Is there a hotel in town?'

'Sure,' the boy replied. 'You could stay at the Sumac. That's Miss Winona's place. She's real nice.'

'Miss Winona only has room for a few guests,' Malloy said. 'Maybe Mr Tulane would be better tryin' the Blue Front.'

'Either,' Tulane answered. 'It doesn't make any difference.' Suddenly he staggered and would have fallen had the boy not been there to steady him. He put a hand to his head and felt a large swelling.

'Funny thing,' the undertaker said. 'There weren't no wound other than that bump.' Tulane winced. 'That and the bruisin',' Malloy continued.

'Don't forget the cut,' the boy added.

Tulane looked from one to the other. 'Are you sure that's all? You checked I ain't got a hole plumb between the shoulder blades?' With a grimace he climbed back into the wagon. 'Maybe you'd better take me to the doc's first,' he said.

Malloy grinned. 'That's easy,' he said. 'Since

Doc Shields up and went, that's me.'

Nobody spoke during the course of the short ride back. Although he didn't feel quite right, Tulane figured there was no point in expecting any help from Malloy. The undertaker dropped him off outside the hotel.

'What about Miss Winona?' the boy said.

'This'll do fine,' Tulane replied. The oldster had chosen to take him to the Blue Front and he didn't feel like arguing about it. He stepped up on to the boardwalk as the undertaker set off down the street. The boy was sitting with his legs dangling over the back of the wagon and he waved as it pulled away. Malloy waved back before entering the hotel. It was a tall building; once he had booked in at the reception desk he was shown to a room on the top floor. Without bothering to undress, he collapsed on to the bed. He lay there staring at the ceiling for a long time until eventually his eyes closed.

When he awoke it was dark. For a moment he couldn't think where he was and he tried hard to recall what had happened to him. He had been passing through Water Pocket on his way to take up a job as wagon boss for an outfit in the Panhandle. One moment he had been riding along, the next he had awoken in his coffin. He could remember nothing of what had occurred in between. He struggled to bring a flickering memory to light, but it faded away. One good thing was that he felt a whole lot better. The sleep had restored him. That, and the surge of well-being he had from being alive.

He got to his feet and walked to the window which gave entry to a narrow balcony. The street was quiet but light and music spilled from the batwing doors of a saloon further up the street. Already he was making plans to find out what had happened to him. The first step would be to pay the marshal a visit and then the Bar Nothing, but that would have to wait till the morning. In the meantime, he could do with a drink; he might pick up some information at the saloon.

It was only as he approached the livery stable on the way there that he thought about his horse. He had been riding a mustang. It had been with him for years, since the time he had cut it from a herd of wild horses. Some folks said that a mustang lacked stamina, but if so, he hadn't ever noticed it. What had happened to it? Had it been brought in with him? The livery stable doors were open and a man sat on a chair in the entrance next to a table on which stood a bottle and a glass. He was tall and lank and smoked a corncob pipe.

'Howdy,' Tulane said.

'Howdy. Mighty fine evening.' The man blew

out a cloud of smoke and peered through it with bleary eyes. 'Stranger in town?' he asked.

'Yup.'

'Thought so. I spend a lot of time observin' folks and I don't recollect seein' you.' He peered closer. 'That's quite a bump you got there. Someone buffalo you?'

Tulane put his hand to his head. 'I don't know,' he said. 'I guess so.'

'I'd have thought a body would recall somethin' like that.'

Tulane peered past the ostler into the stables.

'You lookin' for a horse?' the man enquired.

'I was wonderin' if you got my horse in there.'

A questioning look crossed the ostler's face and was immediately replaced by a light of dawning comprehension. 'Say, you ain't the owner of that black mustang?'

'You got him?'

'Sure.' The ostler got to his feet. 'Come with me.' He led the way as they passed through the stables to an outside corral at the back. 'There he is,' he said.

The mustang was standing among several other horses, but as Tulane approached he tossed his head and came forward.

'How much do I owe you?' Tulane said to the ostler.

'Are you intendin' to take him away right now?'

'No, but I'll be wantin' him tomorrow.'

'You can settle up then,' the ostler said. 'He's a mighty fine horse. It's been a pleasure takin' care of him.'

Tulane held out his hand. 'The name's Tulane,' he said. 'Clay Tulane.'

'Jordan, Jonas Jordan. Glad to make your acquaintance.'

'I was on my way to the saloon,' Tulane said.

'I don't go near the place. But why not join me? I just opened a bottle of whiskey.'

Tulane shrugged. 'Sounds good,' he said. They made their way back through the stables. The ostler pulled out another chair and then disappeared, returning a moment later with a glass and a pipe similar to the one he was smoking. He placed the pipe on the table before pouring drinks. They sat down and each took a swallow.

'That's fine whiskey,' Tulane said.

'Best Joe Gideon. It's sure a lot better than they serve at the Broken Wheel.'

They took another swallow, then the ostler pointed to the pipe. 'Ever tried a corncob?' he said.

'Can't say that I have.'

'Well, I reckon it's about time we put that right. Here, take a smell.'

He picked up the pipe and held the stem. Tulane leaned down to the blackened bowl. The odour was faintly bitter. The ostler took the pipe and filled it with tobacco from a pouch that he produced from his shirt pocket. He handed it to Tulane and, cupping the bowl in one hand, proceeded to light it.

'It ain't new,' he said, 'but so much the better. A new pipe can take a while to break in. I got mine from Boonville, Missouri. I figure they make the best corncob pipes.'

Tulane drew on the tobacco. The taste was like the smell, with an acrid sour tang that complemented the bite of the whiskey.

'I see what you mean,' he said.

He looked out at the dark street along which lights were playing. Behind them, a horse stamped in its stall. The aroma of horseflesh and hay mingled with the haze of smoke. The sense of well-being he had experienced in the hotel seized him afresh. He glanced down the street in the direction of the saloon. The tinkling notes of a piano floated on the air. For a moment he thought of asking the ostler a few questions, but then the thought faded away like the smoke from the corncob pipe. There would be time enough for all that tomorrow. He was content to let the evening take its course.

Jordan broke into his reverie. 'That horse of

yourn,' he said. 'I don't know if you noticed, but it's kinda cut up along the side.'

'Is he all right?'

'Don't get me wrong. It ain't nothin' serious and I tended to him. It's no surprise you didn't see anythin' in this light. But I'd say that horse had been involved in some sort of scuffle. Maybe that's how you came by that bump.'

'What, you figure somebody jumped me and the horse got involved?'

'I don't figure anythin'. But here's somethin' else for you to consider. You got quite a bad cut. From the looks of it, I'd say that could have been caused by a kick.'

'I figured it was caused by a gun butt.'

'Yeah, could be. But it might have been the horse. Maybe both.'

Tulane's brows puckered in concentration as he tried to remember what had happened. It was no use. Instead, he turned his thoughts in a different direction.

'Do you know anythin' about an outfit called the Bar Nothing?'

The ostler inhaled deeply and took swig of the whiskey before replying. 'Sure,' he said, 'Most folks round here know the Bar Nothing. It's one of the biggest spreads in the territory.'

Tulane reflected for a moment. 'Who owns the

17

place?' he asked.

'The owner is called Marsden Rockwell. Seems like he's a mighty ambitious man.'

'Anythin' wrong with that?'

'Nope, not if he operates by the rules.'

'Are you sayin' that the Bar Nothing ain't dealin' fair and square?'

'I'm not sayin' that, but some folks have their doubts. There's been talk of cattle rustlin'. Seems like a lot of his cattle have their ears cut off.'

'What, to remove any other marks?'

'That's a pretty good reason.' Jordan paused to take another drink. 'Why do you ask?'

'A couple of his boys brought me in. I thought I might pay a visit to the Bar Nothing tomorrow.'

'You were lucky they found you,' Jordan replied.

Tulane was reluctant to say anything further about what had happened to him, but he sensed that the time had come to tell the ostler about subsequent events. When he had finished Jordan whistled beneath his breath.

'Hell,' he said, 'Buried alive! That's a new one even for old Skip Malloy. I hope he don't make a habit of nailin' folks down before their time.'

'It ain't an experience I'd like to repeat,' Tulane said.

They were both silent, temporarily lost in thought. Tulane glanced up and down the street.

It was empty now and it came as a surprise to hear the shuffling sound of footsteps. A figure appeared, framed in the doorway.

'Pocket!' the ostler exclaimed. 'What are you doin' out at this time? Does Miss Winona know where you are?'

'It ain't late. Miss Winona don't mind.' The diminutive figure of the boy edged past the door-frame and into the stable.

'Allow me to introduce a friend of mine,' the ostler said. 'This is Pocket. Pocket, this is Mr Tulane.'

'We've already met,' Tulane said. 'Hello Pocket.'

'Hello Mr Tulane. Hope you're feelin' better now. I mean, now that you're not dead any more.'

Tulane grinned and turned to the ostler. 'Pocket was acting as assistant to Malloy,' he explained.

'Oh, I see. Yes, Pocket is a good boy. He some-times helps out here with the horses.'

'Can I have a turn of your pipe?' Pocket asked.

'No. You can't have a drink either, but if you look on that shelf in the corner you might find something.'

The boy ran to the shelf. 'Sarsaparilla!' he shouted. 'Thanks, Mr Jordan.'

'Go right ahead and give the horses a groomin',' Jordan said. 'If that's what you've come for.' The boy made his way to the stalls and they could hear him whispering.

'Pocket kinda belongs to the town,' the ostler said to Tulane. 'His mother died and no one knows who his father was. Miss Winona Purdy – she runs a boarding house – she kinda takes the main role.'

'The Sumac,' Tulane said.

'Sorry? Oh yeah, the name of the guest house. Seems like your memory ain't so bad after all.' Jordan finished his drink and took up his pipe again.

'I tell you what,' he said. 'If you're plannin' to ride all the way out to the Bar Nothing, why not take Pocket with you? He knows the way. He knows most things round here. I sometimes think he knows more than the rest of us. I'd come myself except I got a busy day. Still, you kinda got me intrigued. To tell you the truth, I'd be interested in knowin' more about Marsden Rockwell myself.'

Tulane smiled. 'Sure,' he said. 'If the boy wants to.'

'It'll keep him out of mischief. But have a word with Miss Winona first. The Sumac is right behind Main Street.'

Tulane rose a little unsteadily to his feet and made to hand back the corncob pipe.

'Keep it,' Jordan said. 'I got a few of 'em. Like I said, all the way from Boonville, Missouri. They

20

don't make 'em like that anyplace else.' He called the boy, who came running up to them. 'Mr Tulane is ridin' out to the Bar Nothing tomorrow. How would you like to show him the way?'

'Sure. Could I take one of the horses?'

'I reckon you'll need one if you're goin' to get anywhere. Have you brushed and combed old Dan?'

'No. I'll go and see to him now.'

'You can take him.'

'Thanks, Mr Jordan.'

'I'll come over to the Sumac early tomorrow mornin',' Tulane said, 'and make sure it's OK with Miss Winona.'

The boy looked eager. 'I'm sure glad you ain't dead, Mr Tulane,' he said.

'Yeah, so am I,' Tulane replied. 'See you tomorrow, partner.'

When Tulane got back to his room and had time to think about things, he wasn't sure he had made the right decision to take the boy along with him. He thought he detected the influence of the whiskey both in Jordan's suggestion and his own ready acceptance of the idea. Still, he reflected, it could work out for the best. Pocket knew the area; he should prove a useful guide. His presence might serve to alvert any possible awkwardness in approaching Marsden Rockwell. At the same time, he had to admit to a frisson of excitement at the prospect of paying a visit to the Sumac. All he knew of Miss Winona Purdy was her name but, like Jordan had said apropos of Marsden Rockwell, he was intrigued. He wouldn't have been able to give a reason, but he intended cleaning up his wound and putting on a clean shirt for the occasion.

CHAPTER TWO

Mr Eldon Garrett, attorney-at-law, was sitting at his desk when there was a knock on the door. It opened to admit his secretary.

'Mr Rockwell to see you.'

Garrett hesitated for a moment but before he could say anything the bulky figure of Rockwell appeared behind the woman.

'What's all this? I don't believe in standin' on ceremony,' Rockwell blustered, passing the secretary. He dropped heavily into a chair facing the lawyer.

'Thank you, Miss Fawcett,' Garrett said. The door closed softly behind her and he turned to the rancher.

'We don't often see you in town,' he said. 'I wasn't expecting you.'

'I bet you weren't,' Rockwell said. 'I won't beat

about the bush. I want to know how things stand with my latest offer for the Pitchfork L.'

Garrett shifted uncomfortably in his seat. 'I have put your offer to Mr Loman but I'm afraid his attitude remains the same.'

'Attitude? You mean he's being as stubborn as ever.'

'I have hopes that he might be persuaded—'

'So have I,' Rockwell interrupted. 'I can tell you, I've just about reached the end of my tether with Loman. I intend to adopt a different approach.'

The lawyer looked at him questioningly.

'Time is of the essence,' Rockwell resumed. 'Now I've acquired the stagecoach company, I need the quickest route from Water Pocket to Sageville. And that goes clear across Pitchfork L range.'

'I think that a further offer might just . . .'

'I've made my last offer,' Rockwell said. He sprang to his feet. 'Well, I consider that was a waste of time. I don't expect to be billed for it. Just make sure those papers confirming my ownership of the Valley Line Stage Company are ready when my foreman stops by later.'

'You don't need to concern yourself about that. In fact, I have them ready.' The lawyer rose from his seat, walked to a safe standing in a corner, unlocked it and produced a sheaf of papers. He relocked the safe and returned to his desk.

'There you are, Mr Rockwell. All in order. Certified and legal, you might say.'

Rockwell took them and laughed. 'If you ever get tired of pushin' a pen,' he said, 'you can apply to me for a shotgun guard.' Still laughing, he spun on his heel and stamped across the room.

'Don't bother seeing me out,' he rapped as he opened the door. 'That secretary of yours can do it a whole lot better.'

The door closed on him and Garrett sat down. He remained motionless for a moment staring into space. Marsden Rockwell put some good business his way, but he resented the rancher's arrogant approach. His keen instincts told him that there was more to Rockwell's interest in acquiring the Pitchfork L than securing the easiest stagecoach route and he resolved to find it out. If his hunch was right the information might prove useful.

As Rockwell passed through the outer office he gave the secretary a wink. She looked demurely down but he thought he knew the signal. *Sometime*, he thought. Right now he needed to get to the stage depot. Strange to think the stage line and everything appertaining to it was now his. He owned the stagecoach on which he was expecting Lonnie Spade to arrive.

His lips twitched in an involuntary smirk. Hiring a man like Spade wasn't cheap. You had to expect to pay top dollar for someone with the sort of reputation he had. Maybe it hadn't been wise to let him in on the real reason he wanted the Pitchfork L, but he doubted that he would have gained his services otherwise, even allowing for the money he was paying. Still, if things worked out, there would be money and to spare. If Spade ever decided to get awkward, there were ways of dealing with him.

Yes, his decision to hire the gunman was justified. Lonnie Spade was exactly the sort of man he would need now that lead was about to fly. It was time Loman and the Pitchfork L were brought to their senses and made to see things his way.

The Sumac boarding house was easy to find. Even before the door opened to his knock Tulane could smell the tantalizing aroma of frying bacon. The door was opened by a lady wearing an apron over a checked gingham dress. Her hair was drawn back in a bun, emphasizing the fine high lines of her cheekbones.

'You must be Mr Tulane,' she said in a soft voice which bore a slight southern burr. Tulane was taken aback and she quickly added: 'Pocket has told me about you. You seem to have made an impression.'

'I'm afraid Mr Jordan and I must take responsibility if he got back kinda late last night.'

She uttered a little, rippling laugh. 'No need for apologies. Pocket tends to be a law to himself, but he's got sense. At least, I think so.' She ushered him inside the house. Two doors opened from the hallway and she indicated one of them. 'Would you care for some breakfast? Only bacon, beans and grits, I'm afraid. Oh, and I pride myself on my coffee.'

'That would sure be welcome,' Tulane replied.

When he entered the parlour, he was surprised to find the room empty although two places were set. He took a seat at the table and after a short while the door opened and a man came in. Tulane opened his mouth to speak but something about the newcomer deterred him. The man ignored him and as he took his seat Tulane took the opportunity to observe him more closely.

He didn't like what he saw; the man's appearance seemed to match his manners. He was about thirty years old but his face had a strange, babylike quality about it. It was smooth and somehow unformed and his hair was thin and wispy, like a child's. There was a blankness about his features, an unnerving absence of expression, and the eyes were cold.

Just at that moment Tulane's thoughts were

interrupted as Miss Winona appeared, carrying a tray on which were a breakfast platter and a pot of coffee. She placed it on the table beside him with a smile and then turned to the stranger.

'Yours is coming right up, Mr Spade,' she said.

The man turned a bleak eye on her but his only reply was a faint nod. As she turned away she gave Tulane a look that signalled her own distaste for the stranger. Tulane started in on his breakfast and had almost finished when the door opened and Pocket appeared.

'Ready when you are,' he said, without ceremony.

'What about your breakfast?' Tulane replied.

'I've already had it. I've just got back from takin' Mr Stimson's dog for a walk. Mr Stimson is kinda lame and doesn't get around much himself any more. He's teachin' me to play the banjo in return.'

'The banjo? Well, that's quite somethin'. Why don't you bring it along?'

'Really?'

'Yeah. I expect we'll be stoppin' along the way. You could play me a tune.'

Pocket hesitated for just a moment, glancing towards the other guest before springing for the door. He reappeared, carrying his banjo, at the same moment as Miss Winona came in with the stranger's breakfast.

'Now you aren't going to bother Mr Tulane with that old thing,' she said.

'It's fine,' Tulane replied. 'In fact I suggested he bring it.' He finished the last of his coffee and stood up from the table. 'That was real good,' he concluded.

'Any time,' she replied.

Tulane turned to the boy. 'Come on,' he said. 'It's about time we got goin'.'

Pocket grinned. As they left the room together Tulane glanced towards the stranger but he was preoccupied with eating his breakfast. Miss Winona had disappeared into the kitchen. Tulane hesitated for a moment in the doorway, feeling an odd inclination to follow her and say something, but Pocket had already reached the front door and was holding it open for him. Together, they passed out into the street.

As the stagecoach drew to a halt outside the depot the shotgun guard jumped down and held the door open for the passengers. Rockwell watched closely as they began to alight, but Lonnie Spade was not among them. He felt irritated. What was Spade playing at? He should have arrived by now. He turned away and began to make his way towards the marshal's office. He strode rapidly along, scarcely taking note of the people he passed. He was thinking hard. He would give Spade until the arrival of the next stage. If he hadn't come by then, to hell with him. Spade was only the icing on the cake, after all. With or without him, he was ready to take action against the Pitchfork L.

He continued walking along Main Street and it was only when he reached a corner that he pulled up and realized he had walked straight past the marshal's office. With a shake of the head, he turned and retraced his steps, barely stopping to knock on the door before entering.

The marshal was sitting back with his feet on a table. Immediately he saw Rockwell he swung his legs down and sat up straight. The chair legs scraped on the floor.

'Things busy around town?' Rockwell commented.

'Just taking a break,' the marshal replied. He was a gaunt man with a thin, straggling moustache.

'Don't worry, Keogh. I know you're doin' a good job.'

'Thanks, Mr Rockwell. Nice of you to say so.'

'Yeah. Don't go overdoin' the gratitude though. Fact is, I've got a bit of a favour to ask.'

'Sure. What can I do for you?'

'I think you know how things stand between the

Bar Nothing and the Pitchfork L. I'm afraid to say that Loman is still proving obstinate.' Rockwell paused but the marshal did not respond. 'To such an extent, in fact, that I feel the time has come to adopt more stringent measures. Not to beat about the bush, I intend taking a firmer line.'

'You mean . . .'

'Yes. If Loman can't be persuaded to sell, despite my more than generous offers, he will have to be forced into doing so. That might involve – how should I put it – more physical methods. That's where you come in. Don't get me wrong: I'm not requiring you to do anything that's not compatible with your role as representative of the law. All I'm asking is that you understand the situation. It would certainly be a help to me to know that the law is sympathetic towards the cause of the Bar Nothing.'

A light dawned over the marshal's face. He grinned. 'Go right ahead and do what you think best,' he drawled. 'I got faith in you. The law ain't gonna stand in your way. No siree. You can count on me.'

Rockwell nodded. He reached into an inner pocket and produced a wad of banknotes.

'Here, take this,' he said. 'A little contribution in the name of law and order.'

'Thank you, Mr Rockwell. That's sure appreciated.'

'Glad to support such a worthy cause.' Rockwell started for the door where he stood for a moment with his hand on the knob. 'I'll be in touch,' he said.

The marshal sat still for a few moments after Rockwell had gone before reaching into a drawer and producing a bottle of whiskey and a glass. He poured himself a stiff drink before swinging his legs back up on the table and tilting his chair so that its back rested against the wall. He pulled out a pouch of tobacco and slowly rolled himself a cigarette.

It took longer than Tulane had reckoned for him and Pocket to reach the boundary line of the Bar Nothing. He had begun to have doubts about the boy's knowledge of the terrain when he pointed to a sign swinging from an elaborately constructed wooden frame.

'Looks like a fryin'-pan, don't it?' the boy said.

'Yeah, I guess it does. Or a bit like your banjo.'

They passed underneath the sign and after riding a little further began to see cattle, singly and some in small groups. Recalling what Jordan had said about their ears, Tulane observed them closely but it seemed the ostler was wrong. The ones he saw were earmarked with an underhack.

They continued riding till Tulane drew his horse

to a halt and pointed to something in the distance. 'What's that?' he asked. At first the boy didn't seem to know what he was referring to. 'A long way ahead and over to the right,' Tulane said. 'Somethin' kinda blue and shimmery.'

'Oh,' Pocket said. 'That's Sawn-Off Mountain. It's the only one around here.'

'I guess it's a butte,' Tulane replied. 'Does it lie on Bar Nothing land?'

'I don't know. I don't think so. That way is more towards the Pitchfork.'

'The Pitchfork?'

'The Pitchfork L. It's quite a big spread. Not as big as the Bar Nothing.'

'Who runs it?'

'I'm not sure. I think it might be a man called Mr Loman.'

Tulane allowed his gaze to rest upon the distant butte for a while longer before he turned back to Pocket. 'Have you ever been up there?' he asked.

The boy shook his head. 'No,' he said. 'I ain't never been that way.' He hesitated, looking somewhat uncomfortable. 'Some folks say it's haunted.'

Tulane smiled. 'I guess that's as good a reason as any for stayin' away.'

He had just raised himself in the stirrups to take another look around when his attention was attracted by a group of three horsemen who had appeared behind them, in the direction from which they had just come. The boy twisted in his saddle; he had seen them too.

'Looks like a welcomin' committee,' Tulane remarked. He wasn't surprised; he'd been expecting to be apprehended at some point. So why, as the riders got closer and he had a clearer view of them, did he anticipate trouble?

When they came alongside they drew to a halt and spread out so they were blocking the trail. None of them looked like regular ranch hands to Tulane. He knew the type well. The man who appeared to be their leader gave them a hard stare before he spoke.

'Turn right around,' he growled. 'This is private land.'

'We've got an appointment with Marsden Rockwell,' Tulane replied.

The man regarded him closely through slitted eyes. 'Who are you?' he said.

'The name's Tulane, Clay Tulane. This here is Pocket.'

The man's eyes slid towards the boy. 'Ain't you the young whippersnapper that works for old Skip Malloy?' The boy nodded. 'Thought I'd seen you before.' The man turned his attention back to Tulane. 'I got a feelin' I've seen you somewhere too,' he said.

'Well, I can't say that I recall the pleasure,' Tulane replied.

The man stroked his grizzled chin and looked at his two comrades. They remained stony-faced.

'What business you got with Mr Rockwell?' the man resumed, addressing Tulane.

'That's my affair,' Tulane replied.

A look of anger crossed the man's countenance. He hesitated for just a moment before going for his gun but, quick as he was, Tulane was quicker. Before the man's gun was out of its holster he was looking down the barrel of Tulane's .44.

'Now that wasn't sensible,' Tulane said. Out of the corner of his eye he detected a flicker of movement from one of the other two riders. 'Don't make any false moves,' he said. 'All of you; take your gunbelts off and throw them on the ground.'

With a glance at their leader, the other two began to unbuckle their belts. One of them threw his down but the second man suddenly reached for his gun. Tulane's reaction was instant. As the weapon appeared in the man's hand Tulane squeezed the trigger of his revolver. The man shouted in pain as the bullet tore into his hand and his gun went flying into the air.

'The next one is for right between your eyes,' Tulane said. He turned to Pocket. 'Step down and collect those guns.' The boy sprang from his horse and picked them up before remounting.

'Well, that was all a bit unnecessary,' Tulane remarked. 'Like I said, we're on our way to see Mr Rockwell. I suggest you accompany me to the Bar Nothing without any further ado.'

The three men glowered at Tulane and the boy. Pocket looked up at Tulane with a question in his eyes.

'You better ride on back,' Tulane said.

'But I want to come with you.'

'Yeah, but you can see how things are. I don't think Miss Winona would thank me if I placed you in any more danger.'

'But what about you, Mr Tulane?'

'Don't you go worryin' about me. Just wait for me back at the Sumac. I'll be along pretty soon.' The boy's face showed his disappointment. 'Go on,' Tulane said. 'And when I get back, you can play me that tune on the banjo.'

The boy's expression brightened. 'OK,' he mumbled. He hesitated for just a moment longer before turning his horse and riding away. When he glanced back over his shoulder, Tulane and the three horsemen had already moved on.

As they rode the leader of the Bar Nothing group gave Tulane a concentrated look from time to time. Tulane's attention was fully occupied in watching for any tricks they might be tempted to pull but he was aware that he was the object of the man's scrutiny. Eventually the man gave a loud laugh.

'Hell, I knew I'd seen you before,' he said. 'Leastways, it ain't so much you I recognize as the horse. That's a mighty fine animal.'

'What do you mean?' Tulane replied.

'Hell, ain't you the *hombre* we found lying out on the range the other day with his head bust? I figured you were dead.'

Suddenly he had Tulane's attention. 'Go on,' Tulane prompted.

'Like I said, me and Walbrook found you. Looked to me like you'd been buffaloed.'

'You were the ones who brought me in?' Tulane said.

'Yeah. Me and Walbrook. We left you with Skip Malloy. He's the doc as well as the undertaker. So you weren't dead after all. It must have been a close thing.'

Tulane was trying to assimilate the information. 'So what else do you know about what happened to me?' he said.

'Nothin' other than what I just told you.'

'Now why would you do anythin' to help me?' Tulane said. 'You don't exactly strike me as the carin' type.'

The man paused before replying. 'I don't know,'

he said. 'Ain't you Lonnie Spade? I figured it was a long shot, but Walbrook reckoned there was a good chance.'

Tulane was thinking fast. He had never heard of Lonnie Spade but he had an inkling that it might be to his advantage to play along with what the man had said and pretend to be Spade.

'What made Walbrook think that?'

'Well, ain't you Spade? Isn't that why you were headed for the Bar Nothing?'

The man had obviously either forgotten about Pocket or accounted for him in some way. The presence of the boy might prove hard to explain, but if the subject came up Tulane would think of some reason for having him along. Another thing puzzled him. Why had they been prepared for gunplay if they thought he was somebody Rockwell was expecting? But then it was only now that the Bar Nothing man had made the connection.

'Just keep on ridin',' Tulane replied.

After Tulane had left with Pocket, the house suddenly felt surprisingly empty to Miss Winona. She busied herself washing up the dishes in the kitchen. She hadn't quite finished when the doorframe was darkened as the figure of the stranger appeared behind her.

'Mr Spade,' she said. 'You gave me a start. Is

there anything I can do for you?'

The man grinned. 'Now that just depends on what you're offerin',' he said.

'Have you finished your breakfast? I could make you some more coffee.'

'It ain't coffee I'm thinkin' of.' The man leered. He came forward and stood before her threateningly, barring the way back into the breakfast room. She felt a tingle of fear run down the back of her neck.

'If you'll excuse me,' she said, 'I need to collect those breakfast things.'

The man's mouth twisted in a sneer. She couldn't help observing how black his teeth were. His breath was rancid.

'Sure,' he said, taking a sideways step. 'I'll give you a hand if you like.'

'That's all right, Mr Spade. I can manage.'

He hadn't left her much room and she was forced to brush closely against him. She pushed past into the breakfast room but he was close behind her. She was conscious of his proximity as she bent over the table to collect his tray. As she did so he pressed up close to her and she suddenly felt the pressure of his hands on her breasts. She tried to break free but he only cupped them harder.

'What do you think you're doing?' she managed

to expostulate. She was very scared but struggled to maintain her self-possession. She half-turned to look into his twisted features. Suddenly he let out a hollow laugh before taking his hands away.

'Don't pretend you don't like it,' he said.

She had begun to shake and was trying to stay calm. 'I want you to leave,' she said.

'I can't do that. Besides, I ain't even paid.' He paused a moment. 'I tell you what. Why don't you and I go upstairs and settle accounts right now?'

'Just go,' she said. 'I don't want you in my house.'

'Now that ain't the way to treat a man who's only tryin' to be nice,' he said.

For a moment they continued staring at one another; then, unexpectedly, he laughed again and began to move away. When he reached the door he stopped to glance back at her.

'I ain't finished my business here yet,' he said.

Still sneering, he went through and she heard his boots clumping up the stairs. She sank into a chair and put her head in her hands. Now she was shaking uncontrollably. Biting her lip, she stood up, gathered the dishes and the crockery, and walked back into the kitchen.

Pocket was very reluctant to leave Tulane. He hadn't gone far when he drew his horse to a halt.

He looked back again but there was no sign of Tulane or the other riders. He was impressed with the way Tulane had dealt with the situation. He could certainly look after himself. After a little more thought he concluded that the best thing would be to do as Tulane had suggested. After all, what could he do in a difficulty? He trusted Tulane's assurance that he would be back in due course. With the vestiges of a smile still lingering about his features, he tugged on the reins and continued riding in the direction of Water Pocket.

It was getting along towards the middle of the afternoon when he got back. He had intended making straight for the livery stable but instead he carried on to the Sumac where he dismounted before fastening his horse to a rail. He glanced up towards the house. There was nothing untoward that he could detect but nonetheless he had a feeling that something was not right. Then he saw that the front door was standing slightly ajar. With a growing sense of panic, he walked up to the house, mounted the porch steps and carried on inside.

'Miss Winona!' he shouted. 'Are you all right?'

He paused for a moment, waiting for a reply. The back door was also open and through it he thought he heard the sound of footsteps. He ran to the doorway. At first his eyes could see nothing

41

unusual but then he detected a flicker of movement and he had a glimpse of a figure in the bushes at the bottom of the garden. It quickly vanished from sight and he rushed back inside the house. He heard a low moan coming from somewhere on the top landing and dashed up the stairs. At the end of the passageway he saw the recumbent figure of Miss Winona. She was lying with her head partly propped against the wall. Her clothes were torn and blood was smeared on the wall behind. His heart pounding with fear, he ran to her and knelt down at her side.

'Miss Winona,' he stammered. 'Miss Winona.' He kept on repeating the name. He couldn't think of what else to say or do, then her eyes flickered open and she spoke in a low whisper.

'Pocket? Is that you?'

'Yes, Miss Winona,' he sobbed.

'Now don't upset yourself. I'm all right. But I need you to fetch help.'

He looked at her, his eyes brimming with tears. 'You're head is bleeding,' he said.

'Yes. It hit the wall. But I'll be all right. Is Mr Tulane with you?'

'No,' he replied. 'He sent me back.'

Her eyes closed again but she quickly reopened them. 'Do as I say,' she whispered. 'Go and get some help.' He hesitated, thinking of the shadowy figure he had seen, but she reassured him.

'There was someone but you scared him off. He won't come back. There's no real harm done.'

'But what happened?' Pocket asked.

'Don't worry about that now. Go and get one of the neighbours or Mr Jordan at the livery stable.' She attempted to encourage him with a smile and he got to his feet.

'Don't worry, Miss Winona. I'll be right back,' he said.

He made his way back down the stairs and outside. He kept running, passing several neighbouring houses, not sure where he was going, till he found himself at the livery stable. Jordan was grooming one of the horses and looked up in surprise as the boy came running through the door.

'Hello, Pocket. What's up with you?'

The boy could hardly get his words out. 'Please,' he stammered, 'it's Miss Winona.'

Pocket didn't have to go into further details. Quickly, the ostler realized that something was wrong.

'Come on,' he said, 'Let's get back to the Sumac.'

When they got there, Miss Winona had succeeded in propping herself further up against the wall and had made an attempt at drawing her ripped and shredded clothes about her.

'Mr Jordan,' she breathed, looking up at his approach, 'thank goodness you're here.'

The ostler quickly weighed up the situation. Bending down, he carefully took Miss Winona in his arms and carried her gently into the adjoining room where he laid her carefully on the bed.

'Can you go downstairs and get some water?' he said to Pocket. 'And a towel.'

When the boy had left the room, he turned to Miss Winona.

'Who did this?' he said.

She shook her head as if by doing so she might erase the memory. Then through clenched teeth she replied: 'It was the boarder. Mr Spade. But he didn't get what he was after.'

The boy reappeared and Jordan began to bathe the blood from Miss Winona's head. Trying his best to be discreet, he made a superficial estimate of the woman's injuries but they didn't appear to be as bad as he had at first feared. The main wound was a bad cut to the back of her skull which might have been caused by a bang against the wall. He noticed that her fingers were bloodied and his guess was that she had fought off her attacker and clawed him with her nails. When he had finished she looked a lot better.

'Thanks,' she said, 'and you too, Pocket. I don't know what I'd have done if you hadn't showed up when you did. Just give me a bit of time and I'll be fine.'

'I could send for Malloy,' Jordan suggested.

Miss Winona attempted a smile. 'I don't want any setbacks,' she said. 'Really, he couldn't do anything more. No, like I say, once I've had a chance to rest I'll be OK.'

'Reckon you could do with a strong cup of coffee, though,' Jordan offered.

'Yes, that would be a fine thing.'

The ostler got to his feet. 'Comin' right up,' he said.

CHAPTER THREE

As Tulane and the three Bar Nothing men approached the ranch house, the door was flung open and the figure of Marsden Rockwell appeared on the veranda. He gave the approaching quartet a puzzled look, then his face creased in a broad grin.

'Hey Walbrook!' he shouted to someone inside, 'Come and take a look at this.'

After a moment another man appeared on the veranda. He took in the scene and then burst into a laugh.

'What happened to you, Folsom?' he shouted.

The leader of the three Bar Nothing men scowled. He didn't reply but contented himself with spitting on the ground. Tulane was conscious that the first man's eyes were examining him. He guessed it was Marsden Rockwell. How much did

Rockwell know about Lonnie Spade? He was still uncertain whether to pose as Spade or not. It all depended on whether Rockwell knew Spade. If, as he guessed, Spade was being taken on as a hired gun, it was more than likely that Marsden knew of him only by reputation. That was often the way of it in such cases. A gunman's reputation was his calling card. Arriving at a decision, he acted on it.

'Marsden Rockwell?' he queried.

Rockwell looked up at him. Tulane met his gaze unflinchingly. 'That's my name,' Rockwell replied. 'Who's asking?'

'Lonnie Spade.'

Tulane swung his leg and dismounted. Before he could add anything further, the man Rockwell had addressed as Folsom spoke.

'We found him and a boy trespassin' on Bar Nothing range. He claims he's got an appointment to see you.'

'You didn't do much of a job bringin' him in. In fact, it looks like he brought you in.'

'We were caught out. He got the drop on us.'

'At least you admit it,' Rockwell said.

'I figure he's the same *hombre* Walbrook and me found on the range a few days ago. Do you recognize him, Walbrook? Seems to me we made a mistake ever tryin' to help him.'

Tulane observed Rockwell and Walbrook

47

exchange glances. Folsom's words had caused more than a ripple of interest.

'Well, Mr Spade, now that you finally got here,' Rockwell said, 'I guess you'd better come on in and get acquainted.' He gave a nod to Folsom who with his two companions led the horses, including Tulane's mustang, in the direction of the stable, before turning and going back inside.

Tulane followed Walbrook. When the door closed behind them, Rockwell indicated for Tulane to take his place on a leather sofa while Walbrook made his way to a cabinet at the rear of the room and poured three glasses. He handed one to Rockwell and another to Tulane before taking the third himself and sitting opposite Tulane.

'Well, Mr Spade, what took you so long to get here? I'd been expecting you to arrive before now.'

'I'd say that was pretty obvious,' Tulane replied. 'You just heard what happened to me.'

'Oh yes.' Rockwell turned to Walbrook. 'Do you recognize this man?' he asked.

Walbrook peered at Tulane. 'Guess it could be him,' he replied.

Rockwell seemed to consider his comment for a moment before directing his attention back to Tulane. 'I'm not sure I understood Folsom correctly. Perhaps you'd better give me your account of what happened.'

'I don't know anythin' more than you,' Tulane replied. 'Someone musta bushwhacked me. I got your boys to thank for findin' me.'

'And that's it?'

'I'm tryin' to fit the pieces together myself.'

Rockwell glanced at Walbrook. 'Do you reckon you can throw any light on the matter?' he asked.

Walbrook shrugged. 'I don't know either, but I got my own suspicions.'

'Yes? And what are they?' Rockwell said.

'You know same as me. The way I figure it, the Pitchfork L must be behind it. I reckon they got word somehow that Spade was headed this way and decided to stop him. They lay in wait but something must have gone wrong with their plans. Instead of killin' Spade, they only injured him.'

'How could that have happened?'

'I don't know. Maybe Spade fought back. Maybe somebody disturbed them and they decided to make their getaway. Coulda been me and Folsom; they coulda seen us comin'.' Walbrook turned to Tulane. 'Think hard,' he said. 'Can you not recall anythin'?'

Tulane shook his head. 'Nope. But I think you're right. I figure whoever was involved got disturbed before they could finish the business. I even have a hunch my horse played a part.'

'Your horse?'

'Seems like the cut to my head could have been caused by a kick.' Tulane took a sip of his brandy, savouring it on the tongue. He was no expert, but it tasted expensive. Rockwell continued to regard him closely before speaking again.

'You know something about the way things are fixed here?' he remarked.

Tulane took his time before replying. 'Like I said, my whole memory's kinda vague.'

'I understand,' Rockwell replied. 'In any case, there's no need to go into all that just at the moment. You could probably do with some time to familiarize yourself with the set-up. My foreman, that's Mr Walbrook, will take you over to the bunkhouse and fill you in with the details.'

Tulane was not sorry that the introductions seemed to be over for the moment. He realized he was on very tricky ground. If he could get some further information from Walbrook he would be more than happy. He didn't intend staying around for longer than that. Thankfully, after a few moments Walbrook rose to his feet and Tulane wasted no time in doing likewise.

'Follow me,' Walbrook said.

'I'll see you again in due course,' Rockwell concluded. 'In the meantime, make yourself comfortable.'

Tulane nodded and together he and the foreman left the room. They crossed a yard and continued past the stables till they reached the bunkhouse. Walbrook opened the door. The place was empty but a lot of the spaces were obviously spoken for. Walbrook escorted him to a vacant bunk.

'Hope this is satisfactory,' he remarked.

'It'll do fine,' Tulane replied.

'I'll come back and talk to you later,' Walbrook said.

To prevent him moving away, Tulane produced his pouch of Bull Durham. 'Join me in a smoke?' he said. Walbrook shrugged but sat down on a chair next to the bunk. Tulane took out some tobacco and a paper before handing the pack to the foreman. They rolled a couple of thin cigarettes and lit up.

'Mr Rockwell was sayin' about you explainin' things,' Tulane prompted.

Walbrook regarded him suspiciously. 'All that can wait,' he said.

'Yeah, but I need to get a handle on what's been happenin'. Things haven't been makin' a lot of sense since I got bushwhacked.'

'Well, like I said before, you got the Pitchfork L to thank for that.'

'What's the deal with this Pitchfork L outfit?'

'Take it from me; they're a bunch of low-down coyotes. They've been causin' the Bar Nothing a heap of trouble. Well, the time's come to put a stop to them once and for all. That's why you're here. Believe me, Mr Rockwell has a high regard for your reputation. Now if it was me, I'd have gone up against those varmints long before now. We've got the men to do it. But Mr Rockwell, I guess he's just more patient than I am. Now you're here, though, I figure it won't be long till we hit the Pitchfork good and hard.'

'I see. And you figure the Pitchfork got word I was on my way. How could that have happened?'

Walbrook shrugged his shoulders. 'How should I know?' he said. 'It's only a theory. Maybe I'm wrong. But it sure looks that way.'

Tulane grinned. 'Well,' he said, 'just so long as Mr Rockwell is willin' to pay, I'm ready to fight.'

Walbrook blew a cloud of smoke into the air. 'That's the way,' he said. 'Yup, it's real good to have you on board. I can see we're gonna have a lot of fun puttin' the Pitchfork in its place.' He took another few pulls on the cigarette before standing up and flicking it on the dirt floor. He stubbed it out with the heel of his boot.

'I got to get back,' he concluded, 'but feel free to take a look around. Supper will be ready about six. I'll see you then.'

He turned and made his way out of the bunkhouse. Tulane waited just long enough to finish his cigarette before he too made his exit.

When he got outside he began to stroll away from the ranch house. The sun was getting low in the sky and he was surprised there were not more people about. What had happened to Folsom and his two companions? He was pretty certain, however, that he was under observation. His instincts told him that there was more activity taking place than appeared to the eye, and it was unlikely that Rockwell would allow him to have free scope of the ranch and its environs. He made a mental note of the layout of the place. It might come in useful later.

When he had made a casual survey he bent his steps in the direction of the stables. He had seen and learned enough and he was not willing to take unnecessary chances. Rockwell probably had his doubts about him already, and there was a danger that the real Spade might turn up at any moment. He was hoping that the stable block might be deserted, but it was too much to expect. He was barely inside the building before a dark shape detached itself from the surrounding gloom and took a step towards him.

'Who are you?' a voice snapped.

'The name's Spade. I'm new here.'

The man was closer now. He looked like an old-timer. His lined face was blank. Tulane looked beyond him towards the back of the stables.

'That there mustang's my horse.'

The man's expression relaxed. 'So many new faces around here recently,' he grumbled.

'Is that right?'

'I don't like it,' the man said. 'Time was a body knew who he was workin' with.' He looked Tulane up and down. 'You don't look like some of the others. I figure most of 'em ain't been anywhere near a cattle drive. How about you? You ever trailed a herd of beefs before?'

'Sure. Figure I know the old Chisholm Trail as good as anybody.'

'Ah, the old Chisholm Trail!' The oldster's face creased in a grin. He looked back over his shoulder.

'That's sure a powerful horse,' he said. Together they wandered over to the stall. 'He's been grained,' the man commented.

'That's good. I kinda figured I might go for a ride, take a look at the range.'

'Your saddle is right there on a nail.'

Tulane took it and slung it on the back of the mustang. He had just finished tightening the girths when the doorframe was darkened and another man stepped into the barn. Tulane glanced up. It was Folsom.

'You ain't going nowhere,' he said.

'Ain't that for Mr Rockwell to decide?'

Folsom took a few paces forward and two other men entered the stable behind him. One of them was Rockwell.

'You're right,' he said. 'It is my decision. And I say you stop right here.'

Tulane shrugged. 'Whatever you say.' He bent forward to adjust the saddle and Rockwell spoke again.

'I figure you got some explainin' to do.'

'Yeah? What about?'

'Like how come there are two people claimin' to be Lonnie Spade.'

Tulane hesitated, but only for an instant. Before anybody had time to react, he had swung himself on board the mustang. The oldster moved nimbly away as the horse edged sideways. Digging his spurs into its flanks, Tulane brought it under control and rode straight towards Rockwell and his two henchmen. One of them reached for his gun. Tulane saw a glint of metal but before the man's finger could close on the trigger the mustang had brushed him aside. There were yells from Rockwell's men but Tulane had already cleared the doorframe. He did not pause but, tugging on the reins, headed towards the yard in front of the ranch house.

Shots rang out behind him but they flew wide. Off to his right the door of the bunkhouse sprang open. The building had seemed to be unoccupied but now a couple of men burst through the door. They had obviously been taken by surprise and Tulane was more or less out of range before either of them had the presence of mind to draw his gun and fire.

He was going hell for leather now. He knew that Rockwell's men would soon be coming after him and he was keen to put as much distance as possible between him and the Bar Nothing. He wasn't too concerned that any pursuers would be able to catch him. The mustang was strong and clean-limbed. Once he got going there was little chance of being caught. Besides, he had another plan up his sleeve to evade his pursuers. The only thing that concerned him was the prospect of running into some of the other Bar Nothing ranch hands, and his fears were realized when a bunch of riders appeared ahead of him.

Immediately he changed direction, veering to his left. He glanced behind him. Away in the distance, back towards the ranch house, a gathering cloud of dust told him that the pursuit had got under way from that quarter. The mustang was sweating and foam flew from its nostrils, but

Tulane knew that it was far from spent. Now, instead of carrying on riding hard, he drew back on the reins and allowed the horse to slow. It settled to a trot and then a jog. He could sense the power in its bunched muscles and the urge it felt to carry on running, but he held it in check.

He looked about him. Both sets of riders were drawing much closer. They were coming on at a fast gallop. He could hear the thud of hoofs and the faint shouts of the horsemen. Soon they would be within shooting range. Still he held the mustang back. The men were shouting loudly now and then he heard the first crack of a rifle shot. The moment had come.

With a final glance at the straining horses of his pursuers, Tulane dug his spurs into the mustang's flanks. The big beast responded immediately. Its pent-up energy released, it bounded forward like a thunderbolt. Tulane leaned low over the saddle, feeling the wind part as the mustang tore across the range, its feet scarcely touching the ground. Tulane let out a whoop of sheer exhilaration.

When he glanced back, he could see that the pursuing groups of horsemen were left far in his wake. Their horses had bottomed out and they were reduced to little more than a walking pace. There was plenty of strength and determination in the mustang, but Tulane had accomplished his aim and didn't want to take any chances. Confident now that he was safe from his pursuers, he slowed the horse down to an easy canter.

'Good boy,' he said, and stroked its mane.

He carried on riding for a time. The afternoon was drawing in and soon the light would fade. Eventually he brought the mustang to a halt near a clump of trees and swung down to let the horse rest and feed. Later, he would make his way under cover of darkness back to Water Pocket. Lying down on the grass, Tulane felt in his jacket pocket and produced the corncob pipe Jordan had given him. He filled it with tobacco and lit it, drawing the smoke in deeply. He stretched his legs. On the whole, it had been a good day. He had learned a lot. He figured he knew now just what the situation was into which he had ridden.

Despite the fact that it was two men from the Bar Nothing who had found him unconscious on the range, it seemed the Bar Nothing was the villain of the piece. It looked like Marsden Rockwell was about to wage war on the Pitchfork L and he had been hiring a number of gunslingers to fight his cause. Tulane had been mistaken for one of them. He had a feeling that he and Lonnie Spade were destined to come up against one another and pretty soon, because he had already taken the decision to side with the Pitchfork L. That would be his next port of call.

As he relaxed, he found himself thinking of Miss Winona. Although he had only just met her, she seemed like a nice lady. He guessed that Pocket had made his way back to the Sumac without any difficulty. Sometime, after he got back himself, he would have to listen to the youngster play a tune on his banjo.

Night had fallen on the Bar Nothing. Marsden Rockwell sat alone at his desk looking through some papers. The only illumination was shed by an oil lamp turned low, which cast the rancher's reflection on the darkened window pane. He was not in the best of spirits. Despite his words to Tulane, Lonnie Spade had still not appeared. They had been intended to flush the man out. They had done that but the only result was that the man had made good his escape. Who was he? The uncertainty made Marsden slightly uncomfortable but he was mainly smarting because he had been made to look foolish. Well, he would have his revenge. The stranger might have got away for now, but he would catch up with him soon enough. Nobody outsmarted Marsden Rockwell.

Putting the papers he was reading to one side, he pressed his face to the window and peered into the darkness. He was about to turn back again when he

BACK FROM BOOT HILL

was surprised to see a shadowy figure ride slowly into the yard. At the same moment his foreman Folsom also appeared. The newcomer swung down from leather and while he fastened his horse to the hitch rack, the two of them engaged in conversation. Rockwell sat back in his chair. After a few moments there was a knock on the door.

'Come in!' Rockwell shouted.

The door opened and Folsom appeared. 'A rider just arrived,' he said. 'He says his name is Lonnie Spade.'

Rockwell stiffened. 'Show him in,' he said, 'and stick around yourself.'

Folsom turned and beckoned to the man who was standing behind him. As the newcomer entered Rockwell regarded him closely. He was dressed in black; his guns were slung low and tied with a thong. Instinctively, Rockwell knew that this time he had got the right man.

As he emerged into the lamplight, Rockwell saw that his face was quite badly scratched. Folsom closed the door and took up a position towards the back of the room while Rockwell rose from his chair and advanced to meet the new arrival.

'Mr Spade,' he said, 'we've been expectin' you.' Spade did not reply and Rockwell continued: 'Take a seat. I expect you could use a good shot of whiskey.'

He nodded to Folsom who proceeded to do the honours. Spade barely looked at his glass before tossing back the contents. At another nod from Rockwell, Folsom refilled it.

'Leave the bottle on the table,' Rockwell said.

Spade took another drink and then turned to the rancher. 'I got your message,' he grunted.

'Then you'll know my terms,' Rockwell replied.

Spade turned towards Folsom and glowered at him. 'What's he doin' here?' he asked.

'Mr Folsom works for me. From now on you'll take your instructions from him.'

Spade grimaced. 'When do we get started?' he asked.

'Very soon.'

'I'll need more money on account.'

Rockwell regarded him closely. 'Like I just said, you know the arrangement. However, just to show good faith, you can take this.' He bent down, opened a drawer and took out a small wad of notes, which he handed to Spade.

'I hear you're good,' he said. 'I expect you to prove it.' Spade took the money and stuffed it into a pocket of his shirt.

'From now on,' Rockwell said, 'you take your orders only from my foreman.' He allowed his eyes to rest on Spade's lacerated face. 'You understand my meaning? Anything else you might be involved with is not my concern. But neither is it yours now.'

Spade turned his scowling features on Rockwell.

'It might be an idea to bathe those scratches,' Rockwell said. 'Mr Folsom will show you the facilities and make sure your horse is taken care of. Good night, Mr Spade.'

Spade made as if to say something more but contented himself with finishing off his whiskey before rising to his feet. As Folsom showed him out the door, Rockwell spoke once more.

'Remember, you're workin' for the Bar Nothing now.'

When the two men had gone Rockwell sat down once more at his desk. He had said that Spade's scars were none of his concern, but all the same, he couldn't help but wonder. He didn't like the look of Spade one bit, but he contented himself by reflecting that their acquaintance was only a temporary expedient. Once he had control of the Pitchfork L he could afford to dispense with his services for good and all.

It was late when Clay Tulane rode into Water Pocket, a lot later than he had intended. For that reason he had decided to make his way straight to the Blue Front hotel and wait till morning to call in at the Sumac and check that Pocket had arrived safely back. When he rode past the guest house, however, he was surprised to see lights blazing in the windows. He swung down from the mustang and tied it to the fence before walking up to the door. He knocked and was even more surprised when it was answered by Jonas Jordan.

'Tulane!' the ostler exclaimed. 'Man, am I glad to see you.'

'Why? What's happened?' Tulane began, but before he had time to say anything else there was a rush of movement from behind the door and Pocket appeared.

'Mr Tulane!' he exclaimed, echoing the ostler. 'I knowed you'd be back.'

'Pocket told us what occurred,' Jordan said, seeing Tulane's puzzled expression. 'We were gettin' worried. But don't hang about in the doorway. Come on in. I expect Miss Winona will be pleased to see you too.'

Tulane stepped inside the house.

'Don't be concerned,' Jordan continued. 'There was an incident here earlier in the day but it's all right now. Thanks to Pocket.'

Tulane gave the boy a glance before continuing into the dining room. As he entered Miss Winona herself appeared in the kitchen doorway. Her head was bandaged and she looked a little pale.

'Mr Tulane,' she said. 'I should think you could do with a cup of coffee.'

'Here, let me take that tray,' he replied, taking a step towards her.

'Don't fuss,' she replied. 'I'm perfectly all right.' She looked past him at Jordan and the boy as she placed the tray on the table.

'Take a seat, all of you. I'll be back in a moment.' They followed her instructions and she returned carrying a plate of flapjacks.

'Miss Winona, you shouldn't—' Jordan began to say but she cut him short.

'I made these earlier,' she said. 'So eat up. I don't want to see them wasted.'

With a glance at each other, they took their places at the table. She poured the coffee herself and then handed the plate of flapjacks around. Tulane took one and bit into it.

'By jiminy,' he said, 'this sure tastes good.'

'Miss Winona is famed all round town for her flapjacks,' Jordan commented.

'I don't know about that,' Miss Winona said, and Tulane was surprised to see that her face was slightly flushed. She turned to him and smiled. 'You haven't told us what happened to you at the Bar Nothing.'

'There's not much to tell,' Tulane responded. Quickly, he gave a brief sketch of what had occurred, making sure to tone the whole thing down so as not to cause any alarm. When he had finished he glanced at Pocket. There was a questioning look on the boy's face but, observing Tulane's cautioning expression, he didn't add anything to what Tulane had just said.

'I had a feeling things weren't altogether right between the Bar Nothing and some of the other ranchers,' Miss Winona said. 'But from what you've said, it seems things might be coming to a head, at least so far as the Pitchfork L is concerned.'

'I guess that's their affair, not ours,' Tulane replied. Tulane and Jordan exchanged glances. The atmosphere was warm but the main topic of concern had not been broached. It was Miss Winona who broke the awkward silence.

'You must be wondering exactly what happened here after you left. Well, let me tell you.'

Like Tulane, she wasted few words in recounting what had occurred. 'And that's all there is to it,' she concluded in a steady voice. 'There's no real damage done.'

'It's lucky Pocket got back when he did,' Jordan remarked.

Miss Winona turned to the boy who looked embarrassed.

'Yes. Pocket did well. His arrival was timely. It was enough to scare off Mr Spade.'

'He probably didn't realize it was only a boy,'

Jordan commented.

Tulane had not mentioned Spade's name in connection with the Bar Nothing. He wondered whether he should bring the matter up and decided against it. Later, he might mention it to the ostler. For the moment, however, there was nothing to be served by referring to it. He was angry with himself for having left Miss Winona alone with the man when he left for the Bar Nothing with Pocket. He hadn't liked the look of Spade. He should have trusted his instinctive dislike for the man. Making an effort to stay calm in view of what Miss Winona had said, he vowed inwardly that he would gain revenge for what had happened. His thoughts were interrupted by her voice.

'Pocket, why don't you get your banjo and play us a tune?'

They all looked at the diminutive figure of the boy. Pocket smiled.

'Are you sure? It's gettin' kinda late.'

'Don't worry about that,' Miss Winona replied. She turned to Tulane. 'That is, not unless Mr Tulane needs to get back to the hotel.'

'No ma'am,' he replied. 'I reckon that coffee has freshened us all up.'

Jordan looked at Miss Winona. 'Maybe Mr Tulane could stay on here,' he said. 'He doesn't have to stay at the Blue Front.'

'Yes, that would be real good,' Pocket said eagerly.

Tulane was trying to gauge the atmosphere. He had a feeling that the ostler was speaking for Miss Winona. He sensed that she still felt vulnerable and might appreciate having someone she trusted around.

'Sure, so long as Miss Winona doesn't mind having me as a lodger.'

'I would like that,' she replied, regarding him candidly. Her words were simple but Tulane sensed that they carried more weight than was apparent.

'Then it's arranged,' Jordan said.

There was a moment's silence till Miss Winona turned her attention back to Pocket.

'We haven't forgotten that tune,' she said. 'Go and fetch your banjo.'

CHAPTER FOUR

Dom Loman and his foreman, Hellawell, sat their horses and looked out over the range in the direction of the neighbouring Bar Nothing.

'When do you figure they'll come?' Loman said.

'Soon. Not more than another couple of days.'

Loman's eyes roved across the narrow stream that separated the two ranges. It was in spate but not so as to provide a barrier.

'We've done everything we can,' Hellawell continued. 'The boys are ready. They know what to do.'

'It shouldn't have come to this. A range war isn't what they signed up for.'

'They signed to the brand. You can count on 'em.'

'I don't know. Maybe I should just have accepted Rockwell's offer and sold up.'

'You know that wouldn't have been any solution. The boys know how things stand. They got a stake in all this. They know their livelihoods are on the line.'

'They could find work somewhere else.'

The foreman didn't reply. Instead he turned in his saddle and looked over to where the blue monolith of Sawn-Off Mountain raised its ponderous mass against the skyline.

'You know,' he said, 'I still figure a bunch of cattle could be hid in there.'

'Maybe so. I know you got your theories about those missin' beeves, but we ain't got any proof they were rustled, never mind Marsden Rockwell bein' involved.'

'It would make it a lot easier for him if he had the Pitchfork L. He'd have good access to Sawn-Off Mountain then.'

'That ain't why he wants to get hold of the Pitchfork. Apart from anythin' else, now that he owns the Valley Line Stage Company, he wants the quickest route clear through to Sageville and the railhead east. I won't lie. Things are not lookin' too good. Rockwell has some fast guns on his side and I'm not convinced Lonnie Spade ain't among them.'

'Me neither. I reckon it was always a long shot that the feller Blake and Johnson bushwhacked was Spade in the first place.'

'Well, whether it was him or not, we're gonna just have to accept that we could be in for a hell of a fight.'

With a last long look over towards the Bar Nothing, the two men turned their horses and began the ride back to the Pitchfork L.

Old Jupe Stimson looked out of his window to see the familiar figure of Pocket approaching over the fields at the back of his cabin. Ahead of him the dog romped and played. The old man grinned. Although he couldn't manage to walk the dog himself any more, it gave him pleasure to see the two of them. Leaning heavily on his stick, he moved slowly to the door and opened it wide. The dog came running up to him, jumping at his leg, shaking off drops of water.

'Good boy,' he muttered. 'Good dog. Have you been for a swim?' He looked up as Pocket approached. 'Come on in, boy. I figure you could do with somethin' warm inside you. I got coffee on the boil and biscuits.'

'Could I have a glass of sarsaparilla?'

'Sure, son. Whatever you want.'

They went inside. Pocket sat down with the dog at his feet. The old man came in with a tray on which were glass of sarsaparilla, a mug of coffee and a plate of biscuits.

'Help yourself,' he said.

There was silence for a few moments while they ate and drank. Stimson leaned across and stroked the dog.

'I hear you've been a brave boy,' he remarked. Pocket looked puzzled. 'I heard somethin' about how you came to Miss Winona's rescue.'

'Oh that,' Pocket replied. 'It was nothin'. I didn't do anythin'.'

'Don't run yourself down. We're all real proud of you.' He paused for a moment. 'I gather the man involved was lodgin' with Miss Winona. I think she's goin' to have to be very careful in future. I've noticed some real mean lookin' folk around town just recently. I figure Marshal Keogh should do somethin' about it. I got a theory. I figure there's a nest of the no-good varmints some-where and if I had to say just where I'd make a guess at Sawn-Off Mountain.'

Suddenly the boy was attentive. 'Sawn-Off Mountain?' he repeated. 'What makes you think that?'

'Oh, it ain't anythin' definite. Just a feelin' I got. It's a long, long time since I was ever up there, but from what I can remember the place would make an ideal hole in the wall. It's a mass of canyons and hidden valleys. I'm just puttin' two and two together and maybe comin' up with five, but that's the way I figure it.'

'Mr Tulane said he might take a ride out there. I told him the place is haunted.'

'Who's Mr Tulane?'

'Oh, he's a friend of Mr Jordan. He wanted to visit the Bar Nothing and I showed him the way there.'

'Now that's interestin',' the old man replied.

'Why?'

'Oh, no reason. It's just that I never liked Marsden Rockwell. He's the owner of the Bar Nothing. I figure he ain't to be trusted.' Stimson looked at the boy and smiled. 'Well, that's no concern of yours or mine either. How about we top up that glass of sarsaparilla and then get down to some banjo playin'? I got a new song for you to try. It's a song they sing to quiet the dogies when they're on a trail drive.'

'What's a dogie?'

'What, you don't know what a dogie is?' The oldster stroked his grizzled chin. 'Well, a dogie is just a little calf that his mammy died and his daddy ran off with another cow.'

He got to his feet and moved to the kitchen. Pocket, stroking the dog's head, heard his gruff voice singing tunelessly as he poured the drink.

*

Skip Malloy sat on a chair tilted against the wall outside the somewhat tumbledown building in which he conducted his business. Undertaking was slack. Even when he had a corpse to bury it came back to life. He couldn't help grinning as he thought about the affair with Clay Tulane. Not that there was anything amusing about it at the time. Clay Tulane had every right to be annoyed: furious in fact. However, he had come out of it OK and, he reflected, all's well that ends well. He could do with things picking up, though. For a few minutes he looked back nostalgically at the good old days in Ellsworth, Newton and Dodge City. Ah, the old cow towns. He hadn't lacked for business in those days, no siree. In fact, the sound of shooting was so customary that he put his loss of hearing down to it, at least in part. He had never lacked respect for his customers either, rarely failing to take off their boots and place them under their heads for a pillow. Yes, those were the days.

He was so deep in memories that he didn't realize he had a visitor till he was being shaken violently by the shoulder. He hadn't seen him, never mind hear him. Rudely awakened, he looked up to see the unwelcome figure of the lawyer, Eldon Garrett. He was surprised. He and Garrett moved in different circles and only rarely did their paths cross. The lawyer was shouting. The sounds registered on Skip Malloy as an indistinct babble of sound, sufficient nonetheless for him to be able to pick up the sense of it. By looking at Garrett's lips he could understand what he was saying: he was asking if Malloy could hear him. Just to exasperate the lawyer, he leaned forward, allowing his chair to right itself, and cupped his hand over his ear.

'Can you hear me, old man?'

Malloy strained forward even further, tilting his head as if in a final determined effort to catch the sound of Garrett's voice.

'I say, can you hear me?' Garrett's voice dropped but Malloy's observant eyes registered his final comment: 'Stupid old fool.' He looked enquiringly at the lawyer and shook his head. Garrett opened his mouth and began to bellow again.

'I'm askin' about Sawn-Off Mountain? Do you know anythin' about Sawn-Off Mountain?'

Malloy shook his head again and this time pointed at Garrett's lips. He opened his mouth wide and then pretended to talk in a much exaggerated fashion. After a moment the lawyer began to speak in a similar way, following his example. Malloy was finding it difficult to suppress a chuckle.

'I'm interested in Sawn-Off Mountain. You've been around a long time. Have you ever been up there?'

Malloy looked blank.

'I've heard some stories. Maybe you've heard them too?'

'Stories?' Malloy said. 'You got a story? What about?'

'Not me. I haven't got any stories. I'm talkin' about Sawn-Off Mountain.'

Malloy pointed down the street. 'It ain't me you want to see if you've got a story,' he said. 'You'd be better off takin' it to the *Enterprise.*'

Garrett gathered himself for one last effort. He opened his mouth but then closed it again without speaking. He gave Malloy a withering look and seemed to mutter something under his breath, which the old-timer didn't catch because Garrett began to turn away as he was saying it.

Malloy watched as the lawyer passed down the street before turning a corner. Then he spat in the dust and gave vent to a hearty chortle. When you were old you had to make the most of whatever opportunities life provided for a bit of amusement. He tilted the chair back again and began to build himself a smoke. As he did so, he started thinking. Why would Garrett be interested in Sawn-Off Mountain? There must be something behind it, especially if he had been desperate enough to seek information from an old lag. No doubt he had already tried more obvious sources – such as the

Water Pocket Enterprise. It was worth thinking about further. Who was to say? There could even be something in it for him. In fact, it might be an idea to have a talk himself with his old friend Tad Whale at the *Enterprise.*

Lonnie Spade woke up in the middle of the night to the sound of snores. The bunkhouse smelled of stale leather and sweat. His reception at the Bar Nothing wasn't quite what he had expected and he felt resentful. Hell, who was Rockwell to try and give him orders? He obviously didn't realize just who he was dealing with. He raised his head and then lay back again in the swirling darkness, thinking about the woman at the Sumac and feeling a prick of desire. He had been foiled there too, but he meant to get even. There were plenty of women to be had in any bordello, but this was personal. She needed to be taught some respect.

The more he considered things, the more infuriated he felt. Hell, didn't anyone know who he was? It seemed not. Very well, he would have to teach them all a lesson. By the time he had finished, none of them would forget his name in a hurry. The only question was; how to go about things? Rockwell was offering good money. He already had a wad of notes to prove it. Maybe he should just settle for that, take what he had and light out. On the other hand, there was likely to be plenty more where that had come from.

And then there was the whole business concerning Sawn-Off Mountain. Rockwell had told him enough to whet his appetite. Maybe he'd do better to just stick around. He lay awake for a long time turning things over in his mind before his eyes eventually closed and he fell into a fitful sleep.

Skip Malloy wasted no time, but went to see the proprietor of the *Enterprise* the next morning. Whale was in his office, writing up an editorial, when he was informed of the oldster's arrival.

'Do you want me to show him in?'

'Old Skip Malloy, eh? Now I wonder what brings him here? Sure, I figure I can spare some time for the old buzzard.' He leaned back in his chair as the doorframe filled with the lean shape of Malloy.

'Thanks for seein' me,' Malloy began. 'I know you're a busy man.'

'You don't need to go tryin' to butter me up,' Whale replied, making an effort to enunciate clearly for the oldster's benefit. 'Just say what you got to say.' Malloy seemed hesitant and the newspaperman rose to his feet. 'I got a little something that might help,' he said. He crossed the office to a small cabinet, drew out a bottle and two glasses, and poured a couple of drinks.

'This is good whiskey,' he said, handing one to Malloy. 'Not like the rot-gut you're used to.'

The oldster took a swig. 'Yeah, that sure goes down well,' he said.

Whale raised his glass and took a sip himself. 'Well,' he said, 'Go on. What can I do for you?'

'It's kind of hard to know where to begin.'

'Keep it brief,' Whale prompted.

'OK. I'm here because I was wonderin' if you could tell me anythin' about Sawn-Off Mountain—'

'Sawn-Off Mountain,' Whale interrupted. 'Now there's a thing. You're the second person to ask me that question.'

The oldster grinned. 'Let me guess,' he said. 'The other person; could it have been Eldon Garrett?'

'You ain't as dumb as some folks take you for,' Whale replied. 'In fact, I figure you probably know more about Sawn-Off Mountain then anyone else around these parts.'

'I know somethin'. But the way I see it, you're the man who knows most about the territory. You're the one keeps everyone informed about what's goin' on.'

Whale took another sip of his drink before getting to his feet again. 'Come with me,' he said.

Without waiting he passed through the door and walked across a room where the printing press was being operated. He went through another door and Malloy followed, to find himself in a kind of storeroom, in the back corner of which stood a large cabinet. Whale took a key from his pocket and opened one of the drawers. Inside was a motley collection of files and papers.

'These files contain all kinda things,' he said, 'all the background material we might need when we're writin' things up for the newspaper. You're welcome to take a look. You might find somethin'.'

'Did you do the same for Garrett?' Malloy enquired.

'What do you think? I figure we both feel the same way about that snake-oil seller.'

'Thanks,' Malloy said. 'I appreciate it.'

'Just make sure you put everythin' back where you found it.' Suddenly Whale laughed. 'Hell, what am I sayin'? That stuff ain't been sorted for years. Might as well just throw the whole lot up in the air and see where it lands.'

'Don't worry,' Malloy said, 'I'll be careful with it.'

The newspaperman nodded and walked out of the room. Malloy waited for a few moments before turning hungrily to the contents of the drawer.

He spent some time riffling through the papers and had just about given up hope of finding anything of relevance when he discovered what he was

79

looking for. It could easily have been missed: a grimy page torn from a diary containing two entries. Holding the page towards the light coming in through a dusty window, the oldster screwed up his eyes in order to decipher the faded lettering. The first one read: *Up early to run the sluice. Ran it all day and think we have some gold. Hard work toting dirt but it will all be worth it.*

It was the second entry, however, that really arrested his attention. It read: *I ache from head to toe. Carried out gold to the bottom of the butte. Sawn-Off Mountain they call it. Once I get across the river I ain't never tellin' no one about that mine and I ain't ever comin' back.*

It was with difficulty that Malloy refrained from letting out a whoop. He hadn't been wrong to suspect the lawyer. There was indeed a secret attached to the mountain and he had found it out. Somewhere high in its recesses there was a gold mine and it was a good bet it wasn't worked out. It was no secret that Marsden Rockwell was keen to acquire the Pitchfork L. Folks reckoned it was so he could establish the best stagecoach route; there might be truth in that, but what if he knew about the gold mine? In fact, there was probably a connection. The Pitchfork L rangelands gave the best access to the mountain. Having ownership of the stage line would make it easy to transport any gold there might be. A thought crossed the oldster's mind. If he was right about all this, how did Rockwell know about the gold mine? Maybe there was some further evidence.

He tucked the paper into a pocket and began to delve into the drawer once more. After a few moments his fingers felt another slip of paper which had slid underneath one of the files. He lifted it out; it seemed to be an old newspaper clipping and his heart skipped a beat as he read the words:

A report has reached us of the discovery of gold-bearing quartz in the vicinity of Sawn-Off Mountain. The person making the claim said that he had had a piece of gold assayed at twenty five hundred dollars to the ton. The story, however, seems to us to be entirely spurious and unreliable, more especially as there is no evidence even as to the existence of the above-named individual.

After reading the clipping he leaned against the cabinet, his hand pressed to his brow. The clipping seemed to confirm his suppositions. More than that, it could be the making of his own fortune. He closed the drawer and went through to the print-room. For a moment he hesitated, wondering whether to have another word with the proprietor before deciding that there was nothing he could add. If Whale had known anything about the gold mine, he would have said so in the first place. Besides, it was wise to be discreet. The fewer the people who knew about his discovery, the better. Turning on his heel, he left the newspaper offices and strode purposefully homewards.

When Pocket arrived at Skip Malloy's ramshackle house, he wasn't surprised to see the wagon drawn up and the horses harnessed, but he merely assumed another burial was in the offing. The oldster emerged from the building carrying a heavy sack, which he placed carefully in the back of the wagon before turning to him.

'I won't be needin' any help today, boy,' he said.

'Then what are you doin?' Pocket asked. Malloy watched the boy's lips closely.

'You might say I'm goin' on a little trip,' he replied.

Pocket was puzzled. 'What do you mean?' he said. 'What sort of trip?'

'That really ain't none of your business, but I guess it don't do no harm to tell you. I'm goin' to take a ride out to Sawn-Off Mountain.'

'Sawn-Off Mountain!' the youngster exclaimed. 'But that could be dangerous. There are bad men up there.'

Malloy gave the boy a questioning look. 'Who

told you that?' he rapped. 'Where did you get that idea? Have you been talkin' with somebody?'

'Only Mr Stimson.'

'What? The old feller whose dog you take for a walk?'

'Yes. He's a friend of mine.'

'What did he say?'

'Nothin'. He just told me to be careful because he'd seen some bad men in town. He figured they might be livin' on Sawn-Off Mountain.'

The oldster's mouth moved in an imitation of chewing, weighing up the boy's words. They confirmed some suspicions he had developed following his discussion with Eldon Garrett. It had seemed odd at the time. Why would the lawyer be interested in Sawn-Off Mountain? What Pocket said seemed to confirm that there was more to it than met the eye. If he'd had a vague reason for riding out to Sawn-Off Mountain before Pocket's arrival, he had even more now.

'That's sound advice,' he said, looking at the boy closely. 'You'd do well to bear Mr Stimson's words in mind.' He made to climb up on the wagon seat.

'Can I come with you?' Pocket said.

The oldster halted. 'I don't think that would be a good idea,' he replied. 'You ain't come prepared for a drive. Besides, won't Miss Winona wonder where you are?'

'I don't spend all my time at Miss Winona's,' Pocket replied. 'She's used to me comin' and goin'.'

Malloy turned and spat on the ground. 'I don't know,' he said. 'Mr Stimson might be right after all. It could be dangerous up there.'

Pocket had a brainwave. 'If there's anybody there, you'll need someone to interpret for you.'

Malloy shook his head. 'I'm sorry, son,' he replied. 'I can't deny that it might be useful to have you along, but this ain't a trip for a boy. Give my regards to Miss Winona. I'll see you when I get back.'

With some difficulty he hoisted himself aloft and cracked his whip. The horse jerked forward and began to move down the street. Pocket stood for a few moments watching it, torn between his desire to get back to the Sumac and his curiosity about Sawn-Off Mountain. Mr Tulane had said something about going there one day, but that was too indefinite. Pocket had always wanted to see the place for himself but had been put off because of the stories he had heard. But he was too old to be deterred by any of that now. Here was a great chance to see what the place was really like.

When the wagon had gone a little distance he suddenly burst into a run. Catching up with it, he put his hands on the backboard and jumped. For a few moments he swung precariously before drawing up his leg and tumbling into the back of the wagon. He made some noise but the oldster's deafness was a guarantee that Pocket's action went unnoticed. The wagon was partly filled with a number of items, including a pick and a spade and a couple of rifles, and Malloy had packed a fair of amount of provisions. Pocket wondered what the old-timer expected to find on Sawn-Off Mountain as he made himself as comfortable and invisible as he could.

In the period of time immediately following his return to the Sumac, Tulane was torn between his desire to visit the Pitchfork L and his concern for Miss Winona. Although she put a brave front on what had happened, he sensed that she was feeling nervous and that she appreciated having him around. He didn't expect Spade to put in another appearance. He was pretty sure that he had now found his way to the Bar Nothing. If so, it meant that an attack on the Pitchfork L was imminent. The pressure on him to get to the Pitchfork was growing.

On the evening of the second day following his trip to the Bar Nothing Tulane took the opportunity to talk at greater length with Jordan. He told him in more detail about what he had learned during his short time at the Bar Nothing. When he had finished the ostler let out a subdued whistle.

'How about we have a word with the marshal?' Tulane said.

Jordan's reaction was instantaneous. He laughed out loud and shook his head vigorously.

'Marshal Keogh!' he said. 'I was goin' to say that man's a joke, only it's worse than that. He's probably in with Rockwell.'

'What? You think he's corrupt?'

'Yeah, and so do a lot of other folk.'

'Why doesn't somebody do somethin' about it?'

Jordan shrugged. 'Guess folks just prefer to mind their own business.'

'Until they get involved whether they like it or not,' Tulane replied.

Jordan looked at him. 'Like us, you mean.'

'Us?'

'You've already made a decision to side with the Pitchfork. So have I.'

'Has what happened with Miss Winona somethin' to do with it?'

'Of course. Isn't it the same with you?'

Tulane didn't respond. Instead, he looked around him at the livery stables. 'What about this place? Haven't you got a business to run?'

'It can wait.'

'I'm used to handlin' a gun. Are you?'

'I can use a gun. I just ain't had occasion to do so. Till now.'

Tulane's face suddenly broke into a smile. 'Then it's settled,' he said.

'What do we do next?' Jordan asked.

Tulane took a moment or two to weigh up the situation. 'Seems to me we need to get on over to the Pitchfork L pretty quick,' he said. 'Time's runnin' short. I think Miss Winona is OK now. Besides, Pocket is doin' a pretty good job of taking care of her. I'll go back and spend this evening at the Sumac. I'll have a few words with them both. Be ready first thing in the mornin'.'

'Sure thing,' Jordan replied. They both got to their feet and stood for a moment side by side till the ostler held out his hand. 'Give my love to Miss Winona,' he said.

As Tulane made his way back to the boarding house, he began to wonder whether there might be something between Jordan and Miss Winona. It bothered him a little but he couldn't have said why. By the time he reached the Sumac he had come to the conclusion that they were probably just good friends. After all, they had apparently known one another for a long time. It was no concern of his.

Skip Malloy drew the wagon to a halt. Although he

was enveloped in a blanket of silence, his other senses seemed to have developed beyond their normal range to compensate. Maybe it was a kind of sixth sense that told him something was not right. He stood on the open range and looked about him, first towards the looming mass of Sawn-Off Mountain and then back along the way they had come. Ahead of him was the river and he knew it would be high. Moving to the back of the wagon, he reached in for his rifle. At the same moment something moved and he jumped aside as the face of Pocket suddenly appeared.

'What in tarnation!' Malloy expostulated. 'Pocket! What the hell are you doin' in there? You're lucky I didn't blow your head off.' He had raised the rifle and now he swung it down again.

'Don't be mad at me,' Pocket said.

The oldster gave the boy an exasperated look. 'There'll be time for that by and by', he said. 'Right now, I got other things to think about. Like gettin' across a swollen river.'

The boy climbed over the backboard of the wagon and dropped to the ground beside the oldster. He began to stretch his legs, then suddenly halted. He tilted his head, listening carefully.

'I can hear somethin',' he said.

'Yeah. That'll be the river.' The oldster was angry but his relief at finding that his anxiety had been caused by nothing worse than the boy's presence in the back of his wagon had a pacifying effect on him. He laid the rifle back in its place.

'I should tan your hide,' he said.

'I said I was sorry.'

Malloy shook his head. 'What about Miss Winona?' he asked. 'Won't she be worried about you?'

'She don't expect me to be at the Sumac all the time,' Pocket answered. 'She ain't my ma.'

'All the same,' the oldster replied. He lifted his hand and gave the boy a cuff around the ears. Pocket jumped aside before a second blow could land.

'You're incorrigible,' Malloy said. 'I don't know why any of us bother with you.' A shy grin lit up Pocket's face. 'Well,' the oldster concluded, 'now that you're here, I guess there isn't much I can do about it. Get up in the front seat alongside of me and keep your eyes open for a fordin' place.'

CHAPTER FIVE

As arranged, on the morning following their discussion at the Sumac Tulane and Jordan rode out
of Water Pocket, heading for the Pitchfork L. It
was a dull day. Rain clouds hung low in the sky and
a chill wind bent the grass. On the far horizon
lightning flickered.

'What sort of reception are you expectin' when
we get to the Pitchfork L?' Jordan said.

'What do you mean?'

The ostler grinned. 'Well, I was thinkin' of the
last time you made the acquaintance of some of
their boys.'

'That was all a big mistake.'

'Some mistake! I seem to remember you ended
up in a coffin.'

'Don't remind me,' Tulane replied.

They rode on at a steady pace, putting the miles

behind them. Rain began to fall and they halted to pull on their slickers before continuing. Thunder rolled overhead. Tulane raised his eyes to look for the bulking mass of Sawn-Off Mountain but it was completely obscured by a heavy blanket of cloud. They seemed to have been riding for a long time before Jordan announced that they must be on the outer ranges of the Pitchfork L. Soon huddled shapes of cattle confirmed his opinion, lying with their backs to the wind and the slanting rain. The ground was already heavy under the horses' hoofs. The mustang was big and strong but Jordan's palomino was showing signs of tiring. It came as something of a relief to both of them when they eventually had their first glimpse of the Pitchfork L.

The ranch house was long and low, dominated by the outbuildings behind it. A large shade tree spread its branches over the roof on one side where the ground was slightly raised. What struck Tulane was the strangely deserted aspect of the place. The windows were shuttered and the corrals empty of horses. There was nobody around. They came to a halt.

'What do you think?' Tulane said.

'It don't look normal,' the ostler replied.

They fell silent, reflecting on the situation, till Tulane spoke again.

'Whatever's goin' on down there doesn't affect

what we came here for. We're wastin' time. Let's just carry on.'

Jordan nodded and they started forward again, more than ever alert to the possibility of danger. They rode into the yard and had just dismounted when two figures appeared from an angle of the ranch house, carrying rifles which were pointed at them.

'Hold it right there and throw down your guns,' one of the men rapped.

'We come in peace,' Tulane replied.

'Just do it. And don't think of makin' any fancy moves.'

As they complied the ranch house door was flung open and another man emerged. He advanced to the veranda and looked closely at Jordan before he spoke.

'Don't I know you?' he said.

'Yup, I guess so. And I recognize you.' Jordan turned to Tulane. 'This is Mr Loman, the owner of the Pitchfork L.' He faced the man on the veranda. 'I'm Jordan, the owner of the livery stables in Water Pocket. And this is my good friend, Mr Clay Tulane.'

The rancher looked uneasily from Jordan to Tulane before seeming to come to a decision. 'It'll be OK, boys,' he said. 'Mr Jordan is an acquaintance of mine. You've done a good job. Take their horses and then get back to your stations.'

The two men lowered their rifles and took hold of the horses' reins. As they did so, Loman turned to Jordan.

'Perhaps you'd better come inside out of the rain and tell me your business.'

He led the way and they followed him into the ranch house. It was quite dark inside because the shutters were closed. Boxes of ammunition stood near by and rifles were stacked against the walls.

'Looks like you're gettin' ready for a siege,' Tulane commented.

'That's exactly what we're doin',' Loman replied.

Tulane had thrown out the remark flippantly but he quickly realized that Loman was in deadly earnest. 'It wouldn't be the Bar Nothing you got in mind?' he said.

The rancher turned on him. 'What made you say that?' he asked. 'What do you know about all this?'

'That's what we're here for,' Jordan cut in.

The rancher looked from one to the other. 'Take off your slickers and make yourselves comfortable while I get us all a drink,' he said. 'Then you'd better explain what's goin' on. And if you don't mind, I'll get my foreman Mr Hellawell to join us.'

He poured the drinks and then went out of the room. They could hear him talking with someone. He returned and soon afterwards they heard a back door open and close. A man appeared.

'You want me, boss?' he said. He glanced at Tulane and Jordan.

'Come in. Have a drink,' Loman replied. He made the introductions. 'Mr Jordan and Mr Tulane have something to tell us and I think you should hear.' The tumblers refreshed, he took up his seat again. 'Go ahead, then, gentlemen. We're real interested in what you have to say.'

When Tulane, with help from the ostler, had finished his tale, Loman got to his feet and began to stride up and down the room.

'I knew it,' he said to his foreman, 'I just knew that Rockwell was about to take matters into his own hands.'

'Mr Tulane's story certainly seems to confirm what we already assumed,' Hellawell replied.

Loman turned to his visitors. 'You're sure about wantin' to join us?' he said. 'It seems like Rockwell can muster a considerably bigger force than we can. And he's got hardened gunslicks like Spade ridin' for him.'

'We've made a decision,' Tulane replied. 'Like Jordan said just now, that's why we're here. We're just glad we arrived in time. Rockwell could be on his way right now.'

'Well, I sure appreciate it,' Loman replied. 'I reckon we're gonna need all the help we can get.' Suddenly, unexpectedly, his face creased in a shamefaced grin. 'Oh, and by the way,' he said, 'I apologize for what happened to you, Tulane. Seems like a couple of our boys went too far, assumin' you must be Spade.'

'Kind of ironic isn't it,' Tulane replied, 'that I've got the Bar Nothing to thank for comin' to my rescue.'

'Don't forget the horse,' Jordan chipped in. 'It looks like he might have saved your bacon, wading in like he did and buffaloing you with his hoofs.'

'No thanks to old Skip Malloy,' Tulane said.

Loman chuckled as he resumed his seat. They finished their drinks and sat for a moment in silence. Tulane glanced about him at the stacked rifles and boxes of ammunition.

'We're ready for Rockwell,' Hellawell said, observing him. 'The boys know what to do. They've each got their station. We've assigned some of them to the outbuildings and we've got a lookout to give us a warning.'

'He didn't do a very good job lookin' out for us,' Jordan remarked.

'He's watchin' for a whole big bunch of riders.

Don't worry; he'd soon recognize Rockwell and his crew.'

Tulane looked across at the rancher. 'You've done right to make preparations, but are you sure you want to face up to Rockwell right here?'

'How do you mean?'

'Well, I'm thinkin' you might have done what you can to defend the ranch, but the initiative is still with Rockwell. Besides, you might get cooped up. Rockwell could try burnin' you out or even layin siege to the place.'

Loman stroked his chin before glancing at his foreman. 'Tulane might have a point. What do you think, Hellawell?'

'I'm more used to ranchin' than fightin', but I can see what he's drivin' at.'

Loman turned back to Tulane. 'OK,' he said, 'what would you suggest as an alternative?'

'Durin' the war I learned a few things. One was never to let your opponent dictate terms. Another was to choose the battle site and make sure you had the commanding position. A third was to provide yourself with a way of retreat.'

'Makes a lot of sense,' Loman said. 'Have you got somewhere in mind that would meet with your requirements?'

'This is your spread,' Tulane replied. 'You know the place.'

Loman nodded and looked across at Hellawell. 'What do you think?' he said. 'Can you suggest some location that would suit?'

Hellawell thought for a moment. 'There's the west range,' he said. 'There's some pretty rough country out that way.'

Loman considered the suggestion before addressing Tulane again. 'I don't know,' he said. 'Maybe we should move to the west range. On the other hand, as you said, Rockwell could be on his way even now. We haven't got a lot of time to play with. Maybe we should just stay where we are after all.'

'We've certainly got to act pretty quickly,' Tulane said.

'I think Tulane is right,' Jordan interjected.

Loman's features were drawn. 'This sort of situation is new to us,' he said. 'I just don't know what to do for the best. You seem to have more experience of this kind of thing than we have.'

Tulane finished the last of his drink and placed the glass down. 'Matter of fact,' he said, 'I have been givin' the subject some thought and I've got a suggestion to make.'

'Go ahead. What is it?'

'That big butte, Sawn-Off Mountain. There must be plenty of places up there offering good cover. We could choose a spot where we'd have a clear view of Rockwell's men and be able to retreat if we needed to.'

Loman turned to Hellawell. 'Have you been up there?' he asked.

'No, but maybe someone has.'

Loman's features were tight with concentration. 'We'd be leavin' the ranch house exposed,' he said.

'Rockwell wouldn't destroy the ranch house. After all, he wants the place for himself. Once he finds there's nobody here, he'll soon be on his way again.'

'What makes you think he'd head for Sawn-Off Mountain?'

'You won't get far without leavin' a trail a sugar-foot could follow. He'll come right on after you.'

'Hell,' Loman said, 'I just don't know, so I figure the best thing is to defer to Tulane. Hellawell, round up the men and let them know what's hap-penin'.'

'Sure, Mr Loman.'

The foreman got to his feet and walked to the door. As he opened it they heard the sound of hoofs as a horseman galloped into the yard. Hellawell turned back. 'It's Wilson. Looks like trouble.' He flung the door wide as the rider jumped from the saddle and dashed into the room.

'What is it?' Loman rasped.

'They're comin',' Wilson said. 'They're still aways off but they're comin'.'

Loman turned to face Tulane and Jordan. 'Looks like we're too late,' he said. 'We're gonna have to face Rockwell and his gang right here after all.'

'Yeah,' Tulane replied. 'Better tell your boys to get ready.'

Loman turned to Hellawell and the newcomer. 'Tell the boys to take up their positions,' he snapped. 'Well done, Wilson. You did a good job.' The two men rushed out of the door.

'Where do you want us?' Tulane said.

'I don't know. I figure you know better than me. Do what you think is best.'

Tulane thought for a moment. 'What do you reckon?' he asked the ostler.

Jordan shrugged. 'I agree with Loman. I figure you know best.'

Tulane took another few moments to think before responding. They could hear movement outside and then the sound of feet clattering up the steps. A number of men entered, glancing curiously at Tulane and Jordan. Loman quickly introduced them.

'They're here to help,' he said.

Hellawell was carrying two rifles. 'I took the

liberty of gettin' these from your horses,' he said, handing them over.

The men began to fan out and take up their positions beside the shuttered windows. A few of them ran up the stairs. Tulane watched them for a moment before addressing Jordan.

'Come on,' he said, 'follow me.'

With a nod in the direction of Loman he moved to the door, followed by the ostler. Wilson's horse had been taken to the stables and, looking in that direction, he could see more of Loman's ranch hands taking up their stations. From what he had heard and seen, he was fairly confident that the rancher had positioned his men well, covering most of the ground in front of the ranch house. However, he was pretty sure that Rockwell wouldn't be reckless enough to ride straight in. He would be more likely to come as far as he could while remaining out of gunshot before placing his own men. His idea was to try and outflank Rockwell and to do that he needed to find some more advanced position that would offer cover. He considered the large tree at the side of the building but it wasn't where he wanted to be. He was gratified to see a man already high in its branches. The rising ground just beyond it offered possibilities. The ridge was sufficiently high to conceal anyone behind it.

'What do you think?' Tulane said to Jordan. 'Do you reckon you'd be OK here?'

'Sure, but what about you?' Jordan replied.

'I want to get at them with a cross-fire,' Tulane replied. He looked in the opposite direction. All he could see was a pile of logs next to a water trough with some low bushes near by. He pointed it out to the ostler.

'It ain't much, but it will have to do,' he replied.

'Looks kind of exposed to me.'

'It'll do. It gives me a clear view. No-one would be able to get close without me seein' them.'

Jordan looked back at the ranch house and the outbuildings. 'I reckon you might be in more danger from back there,' he said.

Tulane grinned. 'Most of 'em don't know us. Let's just hope they remember which side we're on.'

The ostler hefted his rifle and moved way to take up his post. From where he was standing, Tulane could not see him. He ran over to the water trough and crouching behind it, began to check his .44s, straining his ears as he did so to catch the first sounds of the approaching riders.

He didn't have long to wait. Soon, he detected a distant rumbling that came and went on the breeze. If he hadn't known that Rockwell and his gang of gunslicks were on their way, he might have mistaken it for a roll of thunder. Involuntarily, he glanced up at the sky. The rain had eased but heavy clouds presaged more to come. He glanced across the open space between him and Jordan but the ostler remained well hidden. He looked back at the ranch house. The windows were open but the shutters remained closed; he knew that at the right moment they would be flung open to release a storm of gunfire from within. Behind the ranch house, the outbuildings gave no indication of the men concealed there.

He strained his eyes to catch a first glimpse of the marauding party but as yet could see nothing. Ahead of him the view was obscured by a fine mist but the drum of hoofbeats was loud despite the muddy ground. Out of the corner of his eye he glimpsed a flash of movement as the man in the tree waved his hat. He had obviously caught his first glimpse of Rockwell's party.

Soon the drumming of hoofbeats was augmented by the creak of leather. Tulane heard voices and horses neighed. The sounds diminished and stopped; Rockwell's men had come to a halt. Tulane had hoped they would advance further, coming within closer range of himself and Jordan, but Rockwell was no fool. It was strange, hearing what was going on near by but not being able to see anything.

Then Tulane caught a flicker of movement and a flash of colour. Some of Rockwell's men were inching their way forward but they were not offering a target. He considered taking a pot-shot but he realized it would be just a waste of a bullet. He would have his opportunity soon enough. Right now he needed to concentrate closely in order not to be outflanked, although he had a pretty good view all round and there was little in the way of cover in the immediate vicinity.

Tulane didn't have time to pursue his thoughts any further, however, because the peace was soon shattered by an explosion of gunfire from Rockwell's men in front of the ranch house. Bullets whizzed through the air above his head, embedding themselves in the ranch house walls. The shutters were flung aside and an answering hail of lead sang through the air. Stabs of flame appeared at all the windows as a barrage of sound battered at Tulane's ears. Smoke billowed across the yard. Shots began to ring out from a position above him and, looking up, he saw the man in the tree pumping away with his rifle. The man shouted something but his words were lost in the general cacophony of noise. He began to wave his arms and Tulane guessed that Rockwell was mounting some kind of offensive. There was a fresh burst of fire in front of him and Tulane caught glimpses of figures moving about.

Raising his rifle and choosing a target, he squeezed the trigger. The man was moving quickly and Tulane had no way of knowing whether or not his bullet had found its mark. It was of little consequence, because he was suddenly involved in a furore of battle. Bullets had been screaming harmlessly high and wide, but now they began to kick up the earth near by. A couple of shots ricocheted from the metal trough and another one ploughed into the water, sending up a hiss of steam. Tulane was firing quickly, pausing only to reload as the rifle grew hot in his hands.

Crouching low, he lifted his head to survey the scene. He could now see some of Rockwell's men moving through the brush towards the side of the ranch house. They were being careless. His rifle jammed and, throwing it aside, he drew his Colts. Drawing a bead on one of the gunmen, he squeezed the trigger. It was a difficult shot, but this time he saw the man fling up his arms and sink to the ground. He fired off another shot but didn't wait to see whether he had hit his target as rifle fire began to crack and more lead came singing close by.

The sounds of conflict grew louder. There was a blast of gunfire from his left and, unexpectedly, Jordan came into view, blazing away. He was taking a big risk and Tulane signalled for him to get back. The ostler was whooping and Tulane could only suppose that he had been caught up in the welter of battle. He signalled again and Jordan seemed to come to his senses, because he ducked down and disappeared behind the ridge.

As if in response, some of Rockwell's gunmen suddenly burst from cover; a couple of them hadn't got far before they went reeling to the ground. The gunfire coming from the ranch house was beginning to prove effective and as a further fusillade split the air Tulane took heart from the fact that Loman and his men were giving at least as good as they were receiving. A shot winged dangerously close to where he was half-sitting, half-lying, and he looked about again for a better position. As he did so he became aware of movement behind him. A figure suddenly materialized and Tulane had already swung his rifle in the man's direction before he realized it was Jordan. Just behind him was another man.

'Hell, you enjoy takin' a risk!' Tulane breathed.

'Never mind that,' Jordan said. 'We need to get out of here.'

'Why? We're holdin' our own.'

Jordan turned to the other man. Tulane recognized him as the man who had been in the branches of the tree. 'This is Wyon,' he said. 'Go on, Wyon. Tell him what you saw.'

'I got a good view from up there. There are more riders comin' this way and I figure they're Rockwell's. They've got a couple of wagons with them. It looks to me like Rockwell's up to somethin'. A group of his men seem to be clearin' some space further back.'

Jordan turned a puzzled face towards Tulane. 'How do you figure it?' he added.

Before Tulane could reply, a fresh burst of gunfire raked the ranch house. When the noise had subsided a little, he turned back to the others.

'I don't know,' he replied. 'Maybe Rockwell is bringin' up those wagons to burn us out. They're probably stacked full of hay or somethin' he aims to set on fire and run into the ranch house.'

'I thought you said he wouldn't want to destroy the place,' Jordan reminded him.

Tulane nodded. 'Yeah. Let's just say I changed my opinion.'

'One thing's for sure,' Jordan said. 'We need to get out of here pretty damn quick. The question is, how are we gonna do it?'

While they had been talking the shooting had dwindled. It seemed to Tulane that Rockwell was perhaps having second thoughts about his abortive offensive. Wyon's words seemed to confirm this. If he was right, it made sense for Rockwell to await the arrival of the fresh men and wagons.

'Loman and his boys were all ready to hightail it for Sawn-Off Mountain till Rockwell decided to put in an appearance,' he said. 'The horses are saddled and ready. Loman's men are still in command of the stables. We just got to get word to Loman and head for Sawn-Off Mountain.'

'Reachin' the ranch house could be awkward.'

'It's a risk we got to take. We should take Rockwell by surprise. He won't be expectin' it.'

'I don't know how many of his gunslicks we've put out of action, but there's probably not too many of 'em near enough to get in a good shot,' Wyon commented.

Tulane grinned. 'Let's hope you're right,' he said. For a few more moments they waited, looking about them, before Tulane gave the word. 'OK, let's go!'

Bent double, they began to run towards the ranch house, darting and swerving as they went. Gun smoke still hung heavy, helping to obscure their movements. All the same, Tulane was expecting lead to be flung at them, but only a few sporadic shots rang out. He guessed that they had either forced the gunslicks further back or they had given up the attack on the ranch until their reinforcements came up. The danger now was that they would be met by gunfire from the ranch house if Loman's men mistook them for some of Rockwell's gunslingers.

They quickly made it to the front yard. A gun boomed twice and bullets threw up dirt but they had reached the veranda without mishap when Wyon staggered and almost fell. A red patch appeared just below his shoulder. Tulane and Jordan grabbed him and as they lifted him up the porch steps the ranch house door opened and Loman appeared, rapidly followed by his foreman. Hellawell was carrying a rifle and as the others helped the stricken man indoors, he opened fire, raking the area in front of the ranch house. When the others were inside he turned and followed them, slamming the door behind him.

'Wyon's been hit,' Tulane gasped. 'Help me get him on the couch.'

While they laid him flat, another man appeared with a medicine chest. Wyon was waving them away, insisting that he wasn't badly hurt. It seemed to Tulane that he was probably right, but they needed to do something to stem the flow of blood.

'What were you doin' anyway?' Loman asked.

Quickly, Tulane and Jordan explained the new situation. 'We need to get out of here,' Tulane concluded, 'and I suggest we light a shuck for Sawn-Off Mountain.'

'We got a couple of wounded men,' Loman

replied, 'apart from Wyon.'

'Are they hit bad?'

The rancher shook his head. 'Nope, just minor wounds.'

Tulane turned back to Wyon, whose shoulder was now bandaged. 'Do you figure you can ride?' he asked.

Wyon's features were drawn but he managed a thin smile. 'Sure. I'll be fine.'

Tulane looked at Loman. 'What do you say? It's up to you.'

Loman was no fool. He could see the sense of what Tulane was suggesting.

'I think you're right,' he said, 'but what about Rockwell? He has the place covered.'

'No, I don't think so,' Tulane replied. 'A few of his men might have worked their way around, but I don't figure there'll be much opposition if we head out the back way.'

Loman nodded. 'Right,' he said. 'Hellawell and I will tell the boys what's happenin'. See you over at the stables. We'll be ready to ride directly.'

Without further ado he made his way out. Most of the men who had been stationed inside the ranch house had already left and they had heard no sound of shooting.

'Seems like the coast is clear,' Jordan said.

'It ain't far to the stables,' Tulane replied. 'But

we'd better not take any chances.'

Tulane and Jordan went to assist Wyon but he waved them aside. They made their way to the back door and peered out. A couple of Loman's ranch hands were just entering the stables but there was no evidence of any of Rockwell's men.

'OK,' Tulane said, 'here we go.'

Drawing his six-gun, he stepped into the open and ushered his two companions past. They quickly made their way across the yard while Tulane kept them covered. When they had reached the entrance to the stables he sprinted across to join them.

Skip Malloy was feeling relaxed. He and Pocket had succeeded in crossing the river and finding their way into the mesa. As they lay with their backs against the wheel of the wagon, enjoying the late-afternoon sunlight, he rolled himself a cigarette.

'How are you doin', boy?' he said. 'The way I see it, you can be pretty proud of yourself. There's not many folks can say they got as far as Sawn-Off Mountain.'

'It feels OK, but what do we do now?'

'We don't do anythin' for the moment,' Malloy replied. 'There ain't no rush. Let's just savour the fact that we're here. Tomorrow we'll start givin' this place a good lookin' over.'

'Are you expectin' to find somethin'?'

'Well,' Malloy said, 'that just remains to be seen.' He glanced at the pinched features of the boy. 'I figure you could do with some grub inside of you,' he said. 'Just let me finish this smoke and I'll rustle us up somethin'.

'Should I start buildin' a fire?' Pocket queried.

'Good idea. It might get colder once the sun's gone down.'

The boy got to his feet and began to forage near by. Every now and again he raised his eyes to look at the surrounding hills. Malloy took a few final drags of his cigarette before flicking away the stub. Standing up awkwardly, he reached inside the wagon for supplies.

CHAPTER SIX

Loman and his men burst from the cover of the stables with Tulane and Jordan in the van. Tulane was braced for a salvo of gunfire but it didn't come. There were a few sporadic shots but they flew harmlessly past. He had been right about the placement of Rockwell's men. He only hoped that his judgement would prove equally sound about Sawn-Off Mountain. They rode hard at first, keen to put some ground between themselves and the ranch house, but soon slowed down so as not to wind the horses. There was no reason to overdo things. Loman and Tulane were united in their opinion that Rockwell would wait for his reinforcements to come up before setting off in pursuit.

'I'd still like to get to Sawn-Off Mountain pretty quickly,' Tulane said. 'Give us time to check the place out and choose the best ground to take on Rockwell.'

'With all the rain we've had recently,' Loman pointed out, 'the river could be in flood. It could make it mighty hard to get across.'

'There's sure to be a ford somewhere,' Tulane replied.

Soon the unmistakable outline of Sawn-Off Mountain appeared in the distance, looking dark and menacing against the cloudy sky. They moved steadily on but it didn't seem to come any closer. As the day wore on the sky began to clear and the mountain changed from dark purple in colour to cobalt blue. No-one spoke. They were preoccupied with what might await them in the recesses of the mysterious butte. Suddenly Hellawell gave a shout.

'Take a look over there!'

They drew rein and turned to where he was pointing. Although the traces were faint, it looked like the grass had recently been trampled.

'Looks to me like some kind of cattle trail,' Loman said. Veering away from the main bunch of riders, he and Hellawell went to investigate.

'It's kinda faded,' Loman said, 'but I'd say for sure that cattle have passed this way. Not many maybe, but some.'

'Interestin',' Hellawell commented. 'Looks like we might have an answer to where those rustled cattle have been driven. It's funny, but I kinda had a hunch they might be stashed away somewhere down this way.'

'And I guess we've got a pretty good idea who's responsible,' Loman said.

'Rockwell!' Jordan snapped.

'You bet,' Loman said. His features were determined. 'Come on. Let's not waste any more time gettin' to Sawn-Off Mountain.'

They continued riding. As darkness fell the clouds finally cleared and the stars began to emerge. Almost without their realizing it, as if it had risen up from the earth, the mountain quite suddenly seemed a lot closer and soon they heard the noise of running water. They advanced to the banks of the river and looked across. The waters were swollen and seemed to offer little prospect of a crossing.

'There's got to be a ford someplace,' Tulane remarked.

Loman was still pumped up. 'Yeah,' he replied. 'And it's right here.'

Without waiting for a reply he drove his horse down the shallow banks and into the water, which quickly came flowing over the animal's flanks. The horse was swimming and the watching men could sense the effort it was making as it strained against the pull of the current, which was carrying them

downstream. Fearing that Loman might be in difficulties Tulane spurred his mustang and splashed
into the river. The water surged around him and
spray was flung into his face. He felt the bedrock
slip away but the mustang was strong. He was
gaining on Loman but the situation was not
looking good.

As the waters deepened Tulane splashed water
into the mustang's face on the upstream side in an
attempt to keep him going in the direction he
wanted. Towards the middle of the stream the
waters were circling in a kind of vortex and there
was danger from debris. A tree branch struck
Tulane's horse and for a few moments he got
entangled in it before the force of the current tore
it away. Looking up, Tulane saw that Loman had
been carried further away.

The situation was becoming serious when suddenly he felt a change as the mustang rallied and
began to rise up out of the river. Its feet had bottomed and as he looked again towards Loman, he
saw that he too seemed to have steadied his mount
and to be travelling in a straighter line. He felt a
surge of relief. The deeper water was not as wide as
he had supposed and they both began to emerge
from the river.

As he gained the further bank, Tulane came
alongside the rancher, who grinned and let out a

whoop. The men on the other side began to cheer as they dismounted. Tulane felt the same surge of elation but was sufficiently aware of the situation to realize how close they had come to disaster.

'What in hell were you doin?' he barked.

Loman was still grinning. 'We got across, didn't we?'

'It was a damned fool thing to do,' Tulane replied. He looked across to the other side of the river. Jordan and a couple of the men were about to enter the river but he waved them back.

'It's too dangerous!' he shouted. 'There's got to be a better crossing. You boys find it and we'll wait here!'

Loman's grin faded and he looked at Tulane. 'Who are you to give orders?' he rasped. 'Those boys ride for me and the Pitchfork.'

'There's nothin' to be gained,' Tulane replied. 'Are you prepared to take the risk of losin' some of them? There's nothin' we can do anyway till mornin'.'

Loman looked about him. Night had fallen and starlight sparkled on the dark waters. Looking across at the men on the opposite shore, he waved his arm in confirmation of Tulane's instructions. They turned their horses and began to ride away along the banks of the river.

'Guess we'd better be makin' camp,' Tulane said

when they had gone.

In response, Loman strode to his horse and mounted. 'You can make camp,' he said. 'I'm ridin' the rest of the way to the mountain.'

'What about the men?' Tulane replied.

'They'll find us.'

Tulane didn't move.

'Come on,' Loman said. 'You've had your way about them crossin' the river. You can let me have my way on this one.'

Tulane hesitated for a moment longer. 'It would make more sense to wait here,' he said.

Loman looked up at the towering mass of the mesa. 'Since when did sense come into any of this?' he said.

Tulane nodded. He made his way to the mustang and climbed into leather.

Although the night was bright, it was dark in the shadow of the butte. Sheer walls of rock towered over their heads as they searched for an opening.

'Are none of your boys familiar with the place?' Tulane asked.

'Nope. Nobody comes this way.'

Loman looked intently along the line of the cliffs. He seemed peculiarly eager to push on.

'Seems kinda strange that so few people have been here,' Tulane continued.

'It's got a bad reputation,' Loman said.

117

'Assumin' they found someplace to cross the river, the rest of the boys should be here pretty soon. I think we should set up camp and wait for them. They'll be able to see our fire.'

'So will Rockwell.'

'Rockwell ain't gonna be here till sometime tomorrow. Besides, he's got the river to cross too.'

'Maybe you're right. Let's just ride a little further and if we don't find anythin' we'll do as you say.'

Tulane shrugged. 'It's dark. We should wait till daylight.'

Loman didn't reply but spurred his horse forwards. Tulane followed. They were both scouring the base of the mountain, looking for an opening, but the walls were unbroken. Suddenly there was a disturbance and something sprang up in front of them. Instinctively they reached for their guns, then Tulane saw what it was.

'It's only a deer,' he said.

The shadowy outline of the deer moved towards the cliff face and vanished as suddenly as it had come.

'Where's it gone?' Loman snapped.

'I don't know. Let's take a look.'

They rode towards the spot where the deer had disappeared behind a corner of the cliff.

'I think we found something,' Loman said.

Beyond the outcropping of rock was a deep cleft in the face of the precipice. Without waiting for discussion, Loman rode his horse into the crevice. Tulane had misgivings but, seeing that Loman was not to be deterred, rode into the cleft after him. It was rough going in the dark but the crevice soon widened. The moon had risen and poured light on to the cliff walls. They rode on into a narrow valley, the trail winding its way upwards. The horses picked their way cautiously. They were both good night horses but Tulane was concerned for their safety.

He was about to say something to Loman when there was a sudden flash of light and a booming crash reverberated from the cliffs. Loman's horse went down, throwing its rider to the ground as Tulane quickly threw himself sideways. More shots echoed round the canyon and both horses went galloping away along the trail.

'Are you hurt?' Tulane said.

By way of reply Loman rose to his feet but Tulane pulled him back down again.

'Don't be a fool,' he said.

'What about the horses?'

'Don't worry about the horses. We can catch them later. They won't go far.'

'Who could have fired those shots?'

'I don't know, but we'd better take cover.'

119

As if to reinforce his words, more shots rang out, striking the ground but not too closely. Tulane observed the stabs of flame on the mountainside.

'I figure there's only one of them,' he said. 'He was probably just lucky with that first shot, but we'd better not take any risks.'

'I don't get it,' Loman replied. 'Who could be up there?'

'I guess we'll find out soon enough. I only wish I'd grabbed my rifle when I left the saddle. Come on.'

There was plenty of cover on both sides of the trail and they soon found shelter. They drew their six-guns and waited, but nothing happened.

'What do we do? Try and make our way back to the entrance to the cleft?' Loman said.

'Yup. I figure whoever took those shots has gone.'

'He might get reinforcements. There could be others.'

'Who knows?'

Loman suddenly blew out his cheeks. 'It could be one of Rockwell's men. We saw that cow trail. Maybe they're hidin' the critters up here some-place.'

'Yeah, that's what I was thinkin',' Tulane replied, 'in which case maybe I was wrong about makin' our stand here. We could have just have ridden into a whole fresh bunch of trouble comin' this way.'

'Let's round up the horses and get back,' Loman said.

Tulane suddenly chuckled. 'You know,' he said, 'I ain't had a chance to give it much attention, but I'm gettin' kinda hungry.'

Carefully, they made their way through the brush to where the horses stood further down the trail with their heads hanging.

'Yours ain't hurt, is he?' Tulane asked.

Loman was running his hand over the horse's hide.

'Nope,' he replied. 'I figure the bullet might have just grazed him or maybe it was the noise scared him.'

They quickly mounted and began to make their way down the trail, watching the sides of the cliffs closely for any telltale signs of ambush. Tulane was fairly certain that their attacker had left and it seemed he was right. They reached the entrance to the cleft without further mishap. Choosing a spot close to the wall of the butte, they soon had a fire going. Loman placed some strips of bacon into a pan while Tulane boiled water in a blackened kettle. While they were eating, they watched out for signs of the others.

The moon was bright and they could see it

sparkling on the river. The sounds of rushing waters were faint but clear. Even allowing for the fact that they were overhung by steep cliffs, it seemed to be peculiarly dark in the immediate vicinity although the landscape beyond was luminous. From time to time they both looked up at the towering, menacing wall of rock above them, conscious of its oppressive presence.

It was only when they had finished the bacon and beans and drunk a couple of mugs of coffee that they heard the sounds of horses and presently discerned the dim form of riders coming towards them from the direction of the river.

Skip Malloy clambered slowly and with some difficulty to the top of the ridge, pausing only once to look behind him. The two riders had taken cover. He could see their horses standing a considerable way off. Then he made his way back down a winding trail to where he had left the wagon and the boy. Pocket was looking anxiously into the darkness.

'I heard shots,' he said when the oldster came up. 'I was gettin' worried. I thought . . . then I figured it was maybe you doin' the shootin'.'

The oldster leaned towards Pocket. He was having some difficulty observing the movement of his lips in the dark. When Pocket had repeated his question, Malloy shook his head.

'Now why would I do that? It would only give away the fact that we're here.'

Pocket looked puzzled. 'What do you mean?' he asked.

'You figure it out. If it wasn't me or those men we saw, then somebody else musta been doin' it.'

Loman and his men had not been the only ones to have observed the cattle trail. Malloy had noticed it too and drawn the same conclusion: that rustled cattle were being driven down to Sawn-Off Mountain. He had observed Tulane and Loman ride towards the butte and assumed they were two of the rustlers. Now he was as confused as the boy. They couldn't have been cattle rustlers. The rustlers themselves must have been responsible for the shots – probably some lookout. So who were the two newcomers?

'Listen carefully to me, boy,' he said. 'I don't know what in tarnation is goin' on here, but it's not how I thought it would be. Things could get mighty awkward. We gotta hide that wagon as best we can and then find someplace to make ourselves scarce till things blow over.' He looked about him. 'There must be plenty of places we can hide.'

'What about the horse?'

'He comes with us.'

Pocket wasn't sure how to react. He felt scared

but at the same time excited. This was an adventure. He trusted the oldster.

'Come on,' Malloy said. 'We got work to do.'

With the coming of dawn, Loman and his cowboys were on the move. The shadow of the butte lay dark and heavy across the landscape and the growing light somehow did little to dispel the gloom. With Loman and Tulane taking the lead, they arrived at the narrow cleft leading into the mesa and entered it, riding in single file. It was dark in the defile but as they rode the canyon broadened. The air was cool but Tulane sensed that as the sun rose higher, it would grow hot. He looked up at the canyon walls, looking for the location of the previous night's unknown gunman. Water was trickling from somewhere high above them. The others glanced about them also, knowing that there was risk of coming under attack.

They rode on for a further mile or so. The canyon continued to open out and the going became easier. Soon they were splashing through a shallow run off; they were following a stream bed which would normally have been dry but was flowing from the previous rains. Just as they were beginning to relax a little the trail took a turn and they were faced a little way ahead by a wall of rock.

'Hell,' Loman said. 'It's a box canyon. Looks like we'll have to turn right round.'

'There's got to be a way through,' Tulane said. 'Let's carry on followin' the stream.'

The way ahead certainly looked blocked but as they approached the rock wall they saw that the meandering waters were fed by a narrow rill which came down the mountainside and seemed to offer a way up.

'What do you think, Tulane?' Loman said. 'You figure we could get the horses up there?'

Tulane's eyes were screwed up in concentration. 'It'll be difficult,' he said, 'but I figure we can do it. At least let's give it a try and see how far we get.'

Loman turned to the others. 'OK men!' he shouted. 'Follow me.' He spurred his horse forward and Tulane closed up behind.

By the time he had found the ford and got across the river, Marsden Rockwell was in a thoroughly bad mood. Loman and his men had escaped his attack on the Pitchfork L and forced him to embark on an unwelcome and drawn-out ride. The arrival of reinforcements had boosted his bunch of hardened gunslicks and they were a size-able force, but he now had the inconvenience of having to track Loman right into the heart of Sawn-Off Mountain. It was getting late. He was faced with a choice: whether to carry on or call a halt for the day. While the last of the bunch were crossing the river, he called Folsom to his side.

'What do you reckon?' he asked. 'Do we press on or let the boys rest up till mornin'?'

'They're gettin' kind of tired,' Folsom replied. 'I figure they could do with a break.'

'It'll be dark soon,' Rockwell muttered. 'It might be difficult to follow Loman's trail.'

'We could head for the line shack. Dravitt and Staunton should be there. Now we've trailed Loman to the mountain, we don't need to worry. There ain't anywhere much he can hide, leastways not for long.'

Rockwell let out a deep sigh. He was in no mood to be making decisions.

'You got a point there,' he said. 'There's nothin' to be gained by rushin' things now. We could set up camp but there doesn't seem to be much point. I figure we'll head for the line camp.'

'I hear it ain't much,' Folsom replied, 'but it's sure got to be better than this.' His glance swept the river and its muddy banks.

'OK. Once the men are over, tell 'em what's happenin'.'

As Folsom rode away Rockwell considered another possibility: abandoning the enterprise and riding back to the Pitchfork L. They would certainly be comfortable there. What was to stop him simply taking over the ranch? It was an appealing idea but he realized he wasn't really thinking straight. A little further thought was enough to persuade him that to do so would only be putting off the inevitable confrontation. Loman would not be content to leave it at that. At some point he would have to come down from the mesa and eventually mount a counter-attack. Better to carry on and deal with him now. His men were prepared and they hadn't come all this way for nothing. To turn round would be to invite dissension. Strike while the iron's hot, he reflected.

As he sat his horse, he became conscious that Lonnie Spade had ridden up near by and his eyes were resting on him. There was something creepy about that man with his baby face and silent ways. He wanted to return the man's stare but made an effort to resist, as if doing so would somehow be a sign of weakness. Instead, he self-consciously reached for his tobacco pouch and began to roll himself a cigarette. He lit up and took a few drags. When he looked again, Spade had gone.

It was a steep climb to the top of the coulee and by the time they had reached it Loman and his men were feeling the strain. The trail levelled off and they came out on a grassy shelf. The men dis-mounted and stretched out on the grass. While they did so, Loman and Tulane carried on riding till they reached just below the final crest. They climbed down from their saddles and inched forwards, taking care not to skyline themselves, till they had a view over the other side. Below them lay a shallow bowl and dotted around were small groups of cattle. They glanced at each other before taking a closer look. For a few moments they could see nothing else, but then they were rewarded with the sight of a small structure away on their right, partly screened by trees.

'Looks like we were right,' Loman said. 'This must be where Rockwell keeps the stolen cattle. They've even built a kind of line shack.'

'There must be other ways in,' Tulane remarked. 'There's no way he could have driven them up the way we've come.'

'I wonder how many men he's got down there? We're already well outnumbered.'

'Not many,' Tulane replied. 'That shack is little more than a hogan. Those cattle are well protected. There's plenty of grass. They can pretty much look after themselves.' He thought for a moment. 'I don't think we need to go any further,' he concluded.

'Why not? I thought we were lookin' for a place to take on Rockwell.'

'I figure we've found it. What could be better

then this? Chances are that Rockwell will head for this place through whatever passage gives access to it.'

'If he follows our trail he'll come up the canyon same as we did.'

'He might well do that, but either way we're in a good position. Just a couple of men could hold this spot.'

Loman nodded, considering Tulane's words. 'I reckon you're right,' he concluded. 'Come on. Let's get back to the others.'

Skip Malloy wasn't taking any unnecessary chances. He unhitched the horse and then, with Pocket's help, set about concealing the wagon. Once he was satisfied that the wagon was well hidden and no one would be likely to find it, he lifted some of the supplies from the back of the wagon and stuffed them into his saddlebags. He took the rifle and stepped into leather, hauling up the boy behind him.

'What are we doin'?' Pocket asked.

'Puttin' distance between ourselves and whoever fired those shots,' Malloy told him. 'And anyone else in the vicinity.' He touched the horse's flanks and it stepped forward. Neither man nor boy spoke further.

The night was clear but the oldster needed to

have his senses about him as they followed a rough path along the floor of a narrow canyon. The horse picked its way carefully and as it progressed the oldster kept looking up at the cliff face. He wasn't sure exactly what he was looking for, but he had seen caves that might offer sanctuary if they weren't so high up.

'I don't like this,' Pocket said. 'I'm scared.'

There was no reply from Malloy. He obviously hadn't heard. Pocket hunched down. He felt cold but he wouldn't have been able to say whether it was the night breeze or his fear of the unknown that caused it. At times they rounded a corner and the breeze blew suddenly louder, echoing round the rocky walls of the canyon like the whispering of ghosts. People had told him that the mesa was haunted and it seemed like they were right. His nerves were on edge but gradually the rhythmic motion of the horse began to lull him. He was just beginning to drift into sleep when he was aroused by a sudden exclamation from Malloy.

'Look! The very spot.'

Pocket could hear the faint sound of running water. Startled, he raised his head and began to look around. They were in an open space; starlight flickered on a narrow stream and in the darkness he could dimly discern a strange structure whose main feature was a large broken wheel.

'There's a mine up there,' the oldster said, pointing to a rock wall. He drew the boy's attention to the wheel. 'That there is for crushin' the rock. They woulda used horse power.'

With some difficulty the oldster dismounted and stretched his legs. After a few moments he reached out a hand to help Pocket down.

'I think we've found a good place,' he said. Pocket was shivering. 'Don't worry,' the oldster continued, 'we'll be safe enough here.'

He reached into his saddle-bags and produced a candle. Then he took the youngster's hand and moved towards the pot-holed cliff face, stopping at the entrance to a tunnel where he bent down to peer inside.

'Can you see anything?' Pocket asked.

Malloy stood upright, struck a match and lit the candle. Again he strove to reassure the boy.

'There's nothing to be afraid of. Just stay close to me.' Taking Pocket's hand again, he stepped forward and led the way into the tunnel. The floor was uneven and led gently downwards. Just ahead of them they could see a rock fall. They continued slowly, planting one foot in front of the other. At intervals wooden struts supported the walls and roof. The atmosphere was musty; when Malloy touched one of the walls there were patches of damp. Beyond the rock fall the tunnel took a slight bend. Shadows thrown from the flickering candle ran along the walls but failed to penetrate far into the darkness.

'We don't need to go any further,' Malloy said. 'Let's go back to the tunnel entrance and see about building a fire.'

The boy's teeth were chattering and Malloy figured the best thing was to get him occupied doing something. When they were back at the tunnel entrance he assigned him the task of collecting some materials together to make a fire just as he had done previously. The boy was tired and hungry. The priority now was to get him warmed and fed and then let him sleep. He would be in a better position to face their difficulties when morning came. There certainly were plenty of them, but through all his worries Malloy couldn't help being buoyed up by the feeling that he had come upon the very thing he was looking for. If he was right, the tunnel they had found must be the entrance to the mine he had read about in the newspaper archives. It was true: he really was on to something.

CHAPTER SEVEN

If Rockwell's mood had been bad the previous night, it was far worse the next morning when his foreman approached him with the news that Lonnie Spade was missing.

'What the hell do you mean, missing!' he shouted.

'Just what I say. His horse has gone. Looks like he decided to quit during the night and rode away.'

'I've paid him good money. What sort of example is that for the rest of the men? Most of them are hired. They don't owe any real loyalty to the Bar Nothing. Hell, this could trigger a whole heap of trouble and disaffection.'

'They know which side their bread's buttered,' Walbrook replied. 'They've come all this way. They ain't goin' nowhere but after Loman. Spade is one man. What difference can it make?'

Rockwell was quivering with rage but he didn't say anything to Walbrook about the real reason for his fury. It had been a mistake to say anything to Spade about Sawn-Off Mountain. Maybe he was wrong, but there was at least a chance that the gunslick had departed not because he simply wanted out, but because he fancied his chances of finding the mine. But then what could he expect to do about it even if he did? Rockwell was slightly comforted by this consideration, but not much. Men like Lonnie Spade were not reasonable. They didn't weigh things up logically. More often they acted on impulse. His suspicions, vague as they were, were not unfounded. It would pay to get moving as quickly as possible to deal with both Loman and Spade. He climbed into leather and gave the signal to ride.

Skip Malloy awoke in a pool of sunlight which flooded into the entrance to the mine. He raised himself up one elbow and looked about for Pocket. The boy was lying beside the ashes of the fire, fast asleep. Malloy rose to his feet and stepped outside to take a look around. At some little distance there was a dilapidated headframe indicating where a shaft had been sunk into the ground. He walked across and peered down it. It was impossible to see how deep it was. He found a stone near by and dropped it down the shaft. After a few seconds he heard a faint splash.

Hell, he thought, *that's deep.*

He wondered whether there might be other shafts. There was no indication of any. Had the person who had written the diary page sunk the shaft? It seemed unlikely. More likely this shaft and the one leading into the cliff face dated from an earlier period and the writer had simply come upon it, just as Malloy himself had done.

Turning his back on the mine shaft, he walked back to the tunnel entrance. The boy was still asleep. Curious to see further into the tunnel, Malloy lit his candle and retraced their steps of the previous night as far as the rock fall. Beyond this point the tunnel was very gloomy but he could see enough to pick his way.

He didn't have far to go before it ended in a small chamber. He held out the candle and instantly recoiled with a shock of fear. Propped against the far wall there was a seated figure. Malloy's instinctive reaction was to turn and run, but he managed to resist the urge. Trying to steady his nerves, he drew in some deep breaths. The air in the chamber was quite fetid. When he had calmed down a little, he drew his gun and edged towards the seated figure. As he got closer the man's face seemed to gleam with a strange pallor and stare back at Malloy with a fierce intensity. Still struggling to steady himself, Malloy saw that it was not eyes that regarded him so fiercely, but the empty sockets of a leering skull.

At once Malloy let out a sigh of relief and began to relax. He was an undertaker. There was nothing unfamiliar to him about a cadaver. He bent down to take a closer look. The skeleton was still dressed in the tattered clothes it had worn in life, which held the bones intact. There was a large hole in the side of the skull. The man had been shot in the head.

Malloy paused to think. The entry in the diary had used the word 'we'. Two men working together had discovered the gold, but only one had emerged to enjoy its benefits. By the dead man's side lay a rusted pick, and when he looked up Malloy could see that the rock wall was rough and pitted. It didn't take a lot of thought to realize that the marks had been made by the implement.

It was then he saw something which really set his pulses racing. Embedded in the rock wall were patches of a different blue-black colour. Malloy reckoned he knew enough to think that it probably contained silver.

Satisfied with what he had found so far, he turned away and began to make his way back along the tunnel. The boy must be stirring by now and he didn't want him to be alarmed by his absence. He stepped by the rock fall, still carrying his guttering candle. Daylight was peering in through the mouth of the cave when it was suddenly darkened by the shape of a man. For a moment Malloy assumed it was Pocket but something about it's form was different. He took a further step before he saw a flash of flame and felt a surge of pain rip through his body. His ears detected only the faint reverberation of a gunshot before darkness flooded over him and he sank into oblivion.

Tulane drew out his field glasses and put them to his eyes. A number of horsemen had appeared, riding down the narrow valley towards them. The early morning sun glanced from their accoutrements.

'Looks like Rockwell finally got here,' he remarked, handing the glasses to Jordan. The ostler took a long look.

'Do you reckon that's all of 'em?' he asked.

Tulane took the glasses again. 'Nope,' he replied, 'There's another bunch right behind. I guess we'd better let Loman know what's happenin' here.'

As if in response to his words the figure of Loman himself hove into view over the crest of the hill. He came sliding down the slope towards them.

'We got trouble,' he said. 'Rockwell's men have arrived and there's more of 'em than we expected.'

By way of reply, Tulane pointed over his shoulder.

'Hell,' Loman said. 'Just what we didn't want. Rockwell is hittin' us on both fronts. We're gonna be mighty thin on the ground.'

'Me and Jordan can handle things here, at least for a time,' Tulane replied. 'They might have the numbers, but they can only ride up here one at a time. We should be able to hold 'em off for a whiles.' He turned to Jordan. 'What do you reckon?'

The ostler smiled grimly. 'Whatever you say,' he replied.

Loman looked unconvinced. 'Get word to me if you need more men,' he said.

Tulane nodded and the rancher went slithering off again. Tulane and Jordan watched him depart before facing each other.

'Well,' Jordan said, 'I figure the time's come to be puttin' your theory to the test.'

Tulane looked away towards the approaching riders. They were getting quite close, riding slowly, their eyes scouring the valley as they rode.

'Just one thing I ask,' he said.

'Yeah. What's that?'

'If the varmint who tried to rape Miss Winona is ridin' with that bunch, leave him to me.'

His words seemed to steel them further to the task in hand. Without further ado, they took up their positions.

The riders came on. They were still out of reach and moving very slowly. They were obviously aware of danger. They had followed the tracks made by Loman's party and they knew that the enemy must be near. The leading two riders were looking closely at the ground. They came to a halt and began to consult with one another.

Tulane guessed they were discussing what might have become of the Pitchfork L men. His lips curled in a slow grin. They were puzzled. Did they know the terrain any better than Loman? Probably not. In all likelihood only a few of Rockwell's inner circle were privy to the cattle rustling. If that was the case, they must be wondering what had happened to the men they were following.

The leader looked up at the mountainside. The track that Loman had followed by the side of the stream offered the only possible way up, but would he realize that? When they got close they should be able to see the sign left by Loman's men, even though they had been riding in single file. How good were their tracking skills? Maybe they would turn round and go back.

139

Tulane licked his lips and glanced across at Jordan. The ostler was on one knee, his rifle raised. Did he realize the horsemen were only just within range? He signalled to the ostler to hold his fire and Jordan gestured back. He seemed to understand the situation. Tulane looked back at the riders. The second group had now come up and the whole bunch were sitting their horses, looking about them, uncertain about how to proceed. Time seemed to slow.

Then the hiatus was broken by the muffled sound of rifle fire coming from the far side of the hill. There was an instant reaction. Jordan's rifle cracked and Rockwell's gunnies began to break up in confusion. Some of them did indeed turn their horses and ride away while others slid from their saddles and took cover. Shots started to ring out but the shooting was speculative.

Tulane held his fire. He watched the scene closely, trying to see if any of the gunmen had moved forward. If they did, they would surely detect that there was a way up the hillside. He saw a flicker of movement below him but resisted the urge to squeeze the trigger of his Winchester. He didn't want to give away their position, although he realized that Jordan's reaction meant it was probably already too late. When he had a momentary glimpse of a figure screened by bushes he guessed that at least some of the gunnies were beginning to ascend the hillside.

'They're comin!' he yelled to Jordan.

He and the ostler had been hoping the gunnies would attempt to ride their horses up the trail; it would have made them easier targets. Still, they were prepared for the onslaught and had command of the top of the climb. It was unfortunate that the outburst of gunfire had commenced when it did. The noise of battle still reverberated from the other side of the hill. Obviously Loman and his men had engaged with Rockwell's gunnies. It was imperative that he and Jordan give a good account of themselves and prevent Rockwell's men from gaining the hill and attacking Loman from the rear.

Tulane strained his eyes but he could not see anyone. He was quickly apprised of their presence, however, when a bullet sang by close to his ear, followed by another which cut a branch from the tree under which he crouched, bringing it down on his head in a flurry of twigs and leaves. As he shrank back, he heard the bark of Jordan's rifle followed by a scream from somewhere near by. He had certainly seen someone and succeeded in getting a good sight on him. The next moment a figure emerged from the bushes below. The man was only visible for an instant but it was long enough for Tulane to loose a shot which sent him spinning backwards out of sight again.

Immediately a furious cannonade resounded from below and Tulane realized that the gunnies had spread out across the hillside. Jordan was blasting away and Tulane followed suit, abandoning his former tactic and pumping lead as fast as he could. Now their position had really deteriorated. Not only had they lost the initiative and failed to keep the gunnies cooped up, but Rockwell's gunslicks knew exactly where they were stationed and that they were only two in number. He and Jordan had done what they could but their situation was rapidly becoming indefensible. His brain was racing, trying to calculate a response.

Taking advantage of a slight lull in the shooting, he glanced over at Jordan. To his horror the ostler was stretched out on the ground. Breaking cover, Tulane began to creep forward. Bullets were whistling by dangerously close and the whine of ricochets sang in his ears. Coming alongside Jordan, he was relieved to see that the ostler was sitting up again.

'It's my thigh,' Jordan said, 'but I figure I can move.'

'That's just as well,' Tulane said. 'We need to get out of here.'

He whipped off his bandanna and bound

Jordan's leg. As he did so the sounds of the surrounding gunfire rose in a new crescendo.

''It might be better to leave me,' Jordan said.

Ignoring the ostler, Tulane helped him to his feet. 'Hold on to me,' he said.

'Why? Where are we goin'?'

'There's only one way, and that's up the hill. We need to try and reach Loman.'

They began to move, bending low as bullets ripped into the trees. Although they were making a strenuous effort, it seemed to Tulane that they weren't making much progress. He was worried about how they would fare once they got beyond the tree line. If any of the gunslicks had managed to outflank them, they would be exposed.

'We're gonna have to make a dash for it,' he said.

Jordan nodded. Tulane looked about them but he could see no sign of any of Rockwell's men.

'OK,' he snapped, 'Now!'

Still keeping low, they began to run. Jordan gasped and Tulane realized what the effort was costing him. The ostler could only limp and it seemed they would never make it to the top of the grassy bench. They were almost there when Tulane heard the scuffle of boots. He swung his rifle to a shooting position, then heaved a sigh of relief when he saw that it was not one of Rockwell's's gunnies, but Loman himself. Quickly seizing up the situation, Loman ran to meet them and placed his arm around Jordan's shoulders.

'Here, let me give you a hand,' he said.

With his assistance they quickly covered the rest of the way. Once over the crest of the hill they paused for a moment.

'Are you sure you're OK for the time bein'?' Tulane asked the ostler.

'Sure,' Jordan answered. The noise of gunfire was getting closer. 'We'd better not wait too long,' he added. 'We need to get out of here.'

Tulane turned to Loman. 'What's happenin' with you?'

'We're holdin' out but we need to retreat and regroup. That's why I was lookin' for you.'

Shots were ringing out from further along the rim and Tulane could see puffs of smoke indicating where Rockwell and his men had taken up positions.

'Come on,' Tulane said. 'Hellawell is rounding up the others.'

They moved forward, helping to support Jordan as they did so. As they progressed the rattle of gunfire dwindled. Suddenly there came a loud outburst of noise from the direction of the line cabin. People were shouting and whooping. They paused to look down at what was happening. The gunslicks were congregating in the yard at the front of the cabin and some of them were looking towards the top of the hill.

'Looks to me like Rockwell and his boys are about to mount a concerted attack,' Loman remarked.

The gunslicks in that particular area were spreading out and a group of them were climbing the hill. Even as they prepared to move on, a fresh volume of shouting burst out and gunshots boomed. Soon gun smoke began to rise from the bushes below.

'Come on!' Loman urged. 'We need to link up with the rest of the boys and beat a retreat.'

They moved forward again. Presently the gunnies in the forefront of the attack appeared. Tulane raised his rifle and squeezed the trigger but the only response was a click. The rifle had jammed. Flinging it away, he drew his six-guns. He felt a bullet tug at the sleeve of his jacket but he carried on, firing now with his pistols. Loman was pumping away with his rifle. The outlaws seemed to halt; at least no more of them were to be seen and there was a lull in the firing. They stumbled on and then Tulane saw a group of men and horses. He recognized them as Loman's Pitchfork L boys. Among them was Wyon with his arm in a sling.

'Good to see you!' he said.

'Quick! Let's mount up and ride!' Loman snapped.

They swung into leather. As they cantered away, they were pursued by a swelling volume of gunfire. It didn't sound too encouraging but as they rode Loman came up alongside Tulane.

'I think we've given Rockwell a real bloody nose,' he said. 'They certainly lost a few men. We might not have finished 'em off yet, but it'll be interestin' to see how many still have the stomach for a fight.'

Tulane nodded. He hoped Loman was right. They would find out soon enough.

Pocket lay on the floor of the tunnel, sobbing quietly beside the inert body of Malloy.

'Cut it out, kid,' a voice rasped. Pocket looked up at the baby-faced stranger but quickly shrank away again. He tried to still his sobs but he couldn't help them.

'I ain't tellin' you again,' Spade rasped. Suddenly he got to his feet and, advancing to the boy, hit him across the face.

'Either you shut up or I do it for you.'

He drew his gun but when the boy succeeded in quietening he slipped it back into its holster. The boy was seriously inconveniencing him but he held back from silencing him once and for all because

146

of a vague feeling that the youngster might prove useful. He looked closely at Pocket.

'What are you doin' with the old man anyway?' he said.

Pocket began to reply but it was a rhetorical question and Spade instantly moved away. If Pocket had known that he was dealing with the same man he had scared off from attacking Miss Winona, he would have been even more scared. He hugged his knees and began to think of her. What he would give to be back safely at the Sumac! The thought of Miss Winona brought the tears back to his eyes and he had to make another effort not to sob and so arouse the ire of his captor.

Spade was looking out of the tunnel entrance. He pulled a tobacco pouch out of his pocket and rolled himself a smoke. He began to pull on it, contemplating what his next move should be. There was a lot to think about: getting back to Water Pocket; dealing with the woman at the guest-house, and now the mine. He was confident that he had found it, but what was the best way to realize its potential? It was a situation he hadn't come across before.

He looked about him. His horse was grazing at a little distance. It was probably a good idea, for the present at least, to get down off Sawn-Off Mountain, taking the boy with him. He inhaled deeply a few times and then, throwing aside the stub of the cigarette, began to move towards the horse when he was stopped dead in his tracks by the sound of gunshots. He had heard them earlier that day but then they had sounded further away. Now, judging by the volume, they were uncomfortably close – no further away than the far side of the hill. There was no doubting who it was. It seemed that Marsden Rockwell was finding Loman and his Pitchfork L boys harder to dispose of than he had imagined.

He stood for a while, listening to the sounds of conflict. Should he leave right now or wait till it was over? He was tempted to move but after further reflection decided that a better idea might be to wait. Despite the impatience he felt to be doing something, he was under no real pressure to get down off the mountain and he didn't want to run the risk of running into Rockwell and maybe getting embroiled in the struggle. No, it would be better to stay just where he was for the moment. Turning on his heel, he strode quickly back to the tunnel entrance.

Once he realized that Loman had given him the slip Rockwell lost no time in gathering his forces and setting off in pursuit. One of the men, named Tyler, who had been left in charge of the stolen cattle, led the way. He realized the mountain better than anyone else; he knew there was only one way that Loman could go and it didn't take him long to pick up his sign. The trail led through another valley but as they rode the trail became narrower. Tyler rode up close to Rockwell.

'We got them now,' he said. 'They're headed into a box canyon. There's no way out for them. We got them trapped.'

Rockwell laughed out loud and waved his men on.

As they rode the sides of the canyon grew steeper and they could see a blank wall of rock looming up ahead of them. The men spurred their horses on, anxious to come up with Loman and finish him off. As they moved forward and the path became even narrower they began to string out. The riders in the forefront, picking up on their leader's enthusiasm, began to shout and wave their rifles in the air.

They were nearing a slight bend in the trail when there was a sudden shout from somewhere above them which rang through the canyon and echoed from the hillsides. It was the signal for a hail of gunfire to rain down on them; too late they realized that they had ridden into a trap. Over-confident and unheeding, they had not thought the situation through. Now all at once an avalanche of rocks began to hurtle down the mountainside on to their heads, each boulder bringing with it cascades of smaller rocks.

They began to panic. Some of those toward the rear started to turn in an attempt to ride back the way they had come. As they did so, they were confronted by a fresh group of horsemen which had come up behind them. It was Tulane and a small band of Pitchfork L men. Loman had divided his forces in two and Rockwell was caught between those on the hillside and the newcomers. At the head of the canyon the avalanche started by Loman and his men hidden among the rocks and bushes continued to roll and crash, spreading further confusion. The frightened horses reared and threw their riders while bullets continued to tear a way through the ranks of the riders.

Then, apart from a few loose stones which continued to bump and roll down the face of the cliffs, the avalanche was over. The riders who had turned to flee back down the trail were met with a further haze of bullets from Loman's men. Down they went but they were too many in number to be stopped completely. Some of them broke through and carried on pell-mell down the trail. Amongst them Tulane recognized the features of Marsden Rockwell. In a flash he had turned his horse and was riding hard in pursuit.

Bullets began to fly past him as a couple of the other riders turned and fired but he ignored them. His whole attention was now fixed on catching up with Rockwell. He knew that the game was up so far as the rancher was concerned. His men were either dead or in flight. There was no likelihood that those who remained would rally to his cause again. They were hired men. The only surprising thing was that they had stuck with him as long as they had.

As if in confirmation, the gunslicks who had ridden away with Rockwell had ceased firing and as the valley widened they split up and went galloping off on their separate ways. Tulane left them to it and concentrated his efforts on Rockwell. The man had a considerable lead over him and it was soon apparent that the horse he was riding was one of the best. It was all Tulane could do to keep him in sight and gradually he began to lose ground.

He had lost track of just exactly where they were heading; somewhere the trail must have taken a bend or a detour because he did not recognize any landmark. Ahead of them loomed a shoulder of rock. Rockwell disappeared around it and when Tulane eventually reached the outcrop, he could not at first see where the rancher had gone. Then Rockwell re-appeared, again riding up the far

slope of a dip in the ground beyond which Tulane
could see some odd structures which he took to be
rock formations.

Tulane spurred his horse onward. The animal
was tiring but he didn't want to lose sight of his
target. Foam flying from its nostrils, the horse
bounded forward. In spite of Tulane's best efforts,
Rockwell continued to pull further away till, unexpectedly, he disappeared again. Tulane carried on
riding and soon saw what had happened. The
ground was badly potholed; Rockwell's horse must
have caught its hoof in one of the holes. It had
struggled to its feet and wandered away, but
Rockwell lay where he had been thrown. He didn't
remain prone for long. He got to his feet and
began to run in an effort to get away from his
pursuer.

Tulane was puzzled as to why he didn't attempt
to reach the horse and remount. Presumably it was
panic which made him simply run blindly. Then
Tulane noticed an opening in the cliff face.
Rockwell must have seen it too because he ran
towards it. Tulane's horse was rapidly fading but
there was no way Rockwell could escape him now.
When he was almost upon the rancher, he flung
himself from the horse, landing heavily on his
target.

They went down in a heap but Rockwell was up

152

first. He swung his boot and caught Tulane under the chin just as he was getting to his feet. As Tulane reeled back, Rockwell drew his gun and fired. Tulane felt the bullet graze his cheek, but instead of firing again Rockwell suddenly took to his heels and ran once more towards the tunnel entrance. Tulane staggered to his feet and set off in hot pursuit. Another shot rang out as Rockwell turned and fired but Tulane was too intent on the chase to think of firing in reply.

Despite his bulk, Rockwell was surprisingly fit and it seemed he might make it to the mouth of the cave; then suddenly he uttered a hideous scream and vanished. Tulane couldn't believe his eyes. What had happened? Where had Rockwell gone? Tulane stumbled on, then drew to a sudden halt within a few feet of an open shaft. There was no indication of its presence, no warning. It was just a gaping hole in the ground. In his blind haste, Rockwell had plummeted down its open mouth. The sound of his scream still rang in Tulane's ears as he peered down the shaft. Only a clammy silence rose to meet him and when he shouted down the shaft, there was no reply. Tulane waited a few moments gathering his breath before shouting again; there was still no reply. He stared down into the blackness. The sides were sheer. There was no way to climb down. There was nothing to be done.

He stood erect, his hands on his hips, still breathing deeply, when he heard a shrill cry. All thoughts of Rockwell were instantly erased as the voice rang out again, calling his name.

'Mr Tulane! Mr Tulane!'

He stiffened to attention. The voice was thin and piercing and he seemed to recognize it. He spun round and was amazed to see Pocket running towards him. Before he could move he saw another figure emerge from the opening in the hillside. Even from a distance it looked vaguely familiar but it wasn't till the man drew his gun that he sensed danger. There was a stab of flame and a loud explosion.

Tulane froze in horror as Pocket went down in a heap, but it was only for an instant. Before the man fired again he had already flung himself forward and was running hard towards him, dodging and weaving as he went. He felt something like a great wave of hate and anger surge through him because of what had happened to Pocket and his senses suddenly seemed preternaturally aware. Looking at the gunman, he recognized the blank baby features as the man he had met briefly at Miss Winona's guest-house. It was Spade. Now he had a double reason for wanting revenge.

Drawing his six-gun, he opened fire. The reaction

was instant as Spade turned and ran, disappearing into the gloom of the mine shaft. Tulane didn't hesitate but carried on impetuously till he reached the mouth of the tunnel. Pausing for only a moment, he flung himself inside. The sight which met his eyes wasn't what he had expected. Spade was sprawled on the floor close to another body which he had obviously fallen over. One of his guns lay near by but the other remained in its holster. He looked up at Tulane's approach and even in the gloom Tulane could see the fear in his eyes.

'Please!' he begged. 'Please, don't shoot.'

Tulane wasn't thinking, straight or otherwise. Something seemed to have got hold of him and to be directing his actions. He realized that Spade must have a reputation as a gunman, but it meant nothing. He knew he was invincible. Seizing the man by the collar, he hauled him to his feet.

'Step outside,' he ordered.

Spade had no choice in the matter. With Tulane close behind, he walked into the sunlight.

'What are you goin' to do?' he whimpered.

'I'm gonna give you a better chance than you gave Miss Winona or the boy,' Tulane replied.

'I don't know what you mean. Who is Miss Winona?'

Tulane didn't reply. Instead he walked backwards,

covering Spade with his gun, till a little distance separated them. Then he stopped.

'You've still got one of your six-guns,' he said. 'Well, let's see just how quick you are. I figure you ain't nothin' but a back-shooter.'

'That isn't fair. You already got your gun in your hand.'

With a deft motion Tulane dropped his gun into its holster. 'Now we're equal,' he replied.

Spade didn't wait. Before the words were out of Tulane's mouth his hand had dropped to his holster. In a mere flash his gun was in his hand but before he could squeeze the trigger Tulane's .44 had already spoken. He staggered back as burning lead ripped into his chest. Tulane fired again. Spade's gun fell from his hand. For a moment his eyes stared back at Tulane but the look of disbelief they contained was instantly replaced by a huge emptiness as he slumped to the ground and lay still.

Tulane stood for a moment as the intensity of his emotions began to fade, to be replaced by blankness and despair as he remembered Pocket. The boy was dead. It seemed like a long time had passed since he had seen him fall under Spade's bullet. Feeling heavy and numb, he turned slowly aside and, in a kind of trance, began to drag himself away from the tunnel entrance.

A strange hush seemed to lie over the scene and envelop him as though his ears had been sealed; then, through the silence, a sound began to make itself heard. Gradually it grew, like birdsong, and through the tears which were flowing down his cheeks he saw something move and advance towards him. Suddenly he seemed to come to his senses and he saw that the moving object was just a boy waving his arms and shouting:

'Mr Tulane! Mr Tulane!'

His heart thumped and something warm flooded his chest. It was Pocket! The boy was not dead but alive! At once laughing and crying, he ran forward to take him in his arms and embrace him.

'Pocket,' he stammered. 'Pocket. Are you sure you're not hurt? I saw you fall. I thought . . .'

'I tripped over something trying to get away from that man. I was so pleased when you turned up. I ran out of the cave before he could stop me.'

Tulane took the boy's hand. 'We'd better get you away from here,' he said.

Pocket turned his face up to Tulane's. 'But what about Mr Malloy?' he said. 'We can't leave Mr Malloy.'

'Malloy?' Tulane was more puzzled than ever. 'What has Malloy got to do with anythin'?'

Before the boy could reply, Tulane knew that

Malloy must be the other person he had seen slumped in the tunnel.

'You wait here,' he said. 'I'll go see about Malloy.'

He turned to go back but Pocket detained him. 'Mr Tulane, you're bleedin',' he said.

Tulane looked down. A large red stain had spread across his shirt. He realized for the first time that he had been hit in the side. The bullet he had assumed was aimed at Pocket had been aimed at him. He knew instinctively that it wasn't a bad wound.

'It's nothin',' he said.

'Be careful,' Pocket said.

Tulane nodded and made his way to the tunnel entrance. Kneeling beside the prostrate figure, he recognized Malloy. He felt for a pulse and found one. Even as he examined the oldster, one eye flickered open.

'Is that you, Tulane?' he murmured.

'You've taken a bullet in the leg and your head's cut. I figure you must have knocked yourself out when you fell.'

'The boy,' Malloy said. 'Where's the boy?'

'You mean Pocket? He's fine. Now just take it easy while I figure a way to get all of us out of here.'

Over a week had gone by. Loman and his men had returned to the Pitchfork L, driving the missing

158

cattle with them. Tulane, Jordan and Pocket had stayed on for a few days while the oldster recovered. Since he was the only person passing as a doctor in town, there was something of a problem till it emerged that Hellawell knew enough medicine to dig out the bullets Malloy and Tulane had taken. Neither of them was badly hurt, although it was likely that Malloy would be left with a limp to go alongside his other ailments. Loman was full of gratitude for the help Tulane and Jordan had provided.

'Any time you need a job,' he said to Tulane, 'there's one right here. I don't reckon we'd have come through this without you.'

'Rockwell should never have been allowed to get as far as he did. What about the law around town?'

Loman smiled. 'Well, that's another question altogether,' he said. 'Still, one thing's for sure. Now that Rockwell's out of the picture, Marshal Keogh won't be stayin' long in place. Maybe things will be different when we get somebody who's up to the job.'

Tulane was silent for a few moments, thinking about the rancher's offer. 'You know,' he concluded. 'I might just take you up on that.'

When Malloy was fit to be moved, Tulane and Jordan, together with Pocket, made their way back to town. On a balmy evening they all sat around the table at the Sumac guest-house, relaxing and talking after Miss Winona had served them all a slap-up meal.

'You're welcome to stay here as long as you like,' Miss Winona said to Tulane.

'At reduced rates?' Jordan joked.

Tulane, observing her, thought he saw a faint blush rise to her cheeks.

'It's much appreciated, ma'am,' he replied. 'I'd be glad to put up here for a while.'

Pocket looked eagerly from one to the other. 'It'll be great havin' Mr Tulane around,' he said to all and sundry.

'Maybe you can teach me that old banjo,' Tulane remarked.

'What do you think will become of the mine?' Jordan said.

Tulane shrugged. 'I don't know and I don't care. I guess someone might have a legal claim. I guess the same goes for the Bar Nothing. Best leave that to the lawyers.'

'It could be the making of Water Pocket,' Jordan replied. 'If there's gold still left.'

Miss Winona shook her head. 'I don't know,' she said. 'If it attracts gold seekers, I'm not sure that's a good thing. I kinda like Water Pocket just the way it is.'

She and Tulane exchanged glances.

'Me too,' Tulane said.

This book is to be returned on or before the last date stamped below